DRAWN
into LOVE

Shooting Stars Series

Fighting to Breathe
Wide Open Spaces
One Last Wish

Fluke My Life Series

Running into Love
Stumbling into Love
Tossed into Love

Ruby Falls Series

Falling Fast

Writing as C. A Rose

Alfha Law Series

Justified
Liability
Verdict (coming soon)

Stand-Alone Titles

Finders Keepers

DRAWN
into LOVE

Aurora Rose Reynolds

Montlake
Romance

Text copyright © 2019 by Crystal Aurora Rose Reynolds

Published by Montlake Romance, Seattle

www.apub.com

Amazon, the Amazon logo, and Montlake Romance are trademarks of Amazon.com, Inc., or its affiliates.

ISBN-13: 9781542041737
ISBN-10: 1542041732

Cover design by Letitia Hasser

Cover photography by Sara Eirew

Printed in the United States of America

To the Montlake team. Thank you for all you've done. Thank you for believing in me and this series.

Chapter 1

New Foundation

Courtney

After a sip of wine, I pick up the packing tape and close up another box. Leaning back on my heels, I look around my almost-empty living room. Who would have thought that six years of someone's life could fit into a few cardboard boxes? The proof is stacked up against the wall, waiting for the movers, who will be here in the morning. The house phone rings in the kitchen, causing me to sigh. Only two people call the house line: my former mother-in-law and my ex-husband. The voice mail kicks on, and I cringe as my ex-husband's voice echoes through the quiet house.

"Courtney, it's Tom. I spoke with Mom. She said that the movers are coming tomorrow morning. I was wondering if you'd like to get dinner tonight. We should talk before you leave. Call me back."

A loud beep fills the air. When I look down, I notice that my nails are digging into my palms. Talk? It's funny that he always wants to talk now. Whenever I tried to talk to him during the last two years of our marriage, he was always too busy, always telling me that we didn't have anything to talk about, that everything was fine. But everything *wasn't* fine, because I found out he was a cheating jerk who knocked up his secretary while I was going through fertility treatments in hope of giving us the family we had talked about for years. I unclench my fists and pick up my wineglass, gulping the rest down before heading to the kitchen.

Once there, I turn on the faucet and fill the glass as I look through the window above the sink. I used to love standing right here and day-dreaming about the day I'd see my children playing in the yard. This house was full of those kinds of dreams—dreams that kept me going when nothing else would. When Tom and I bought this house, we were young and in love, excited about the future, excited about our future together. I was twenty-three when we met. I had just moved to Boston from Albany, and I'd started working as a paralegal for a law firm downtown, where he was a lawyer. I don't really remember how we got together, but I do know what drew me to him. He had a big, close family—something I had always wanted. He also seemed to have compassion for others who were less fortunate, which was a rare quality in the men I knew back then. When we met, he seemed like everything I had been looking for: he was kind and stable and accepted everything about me. Growing up in the foster system, I never had a solid founda-tion or anyone to lean on when times were difficult. He gave me those things. Well, he gave them to me for a while, anyway.

"It's time to build your own foundation," I remind myself out loud as I shut off the water and head toward the living room to finish packing.

Tomorrow I start my new life. Tomorrow I will be moving out of this house and to New York City, where I have a job lined up at a law firm that specializes in divorce. It's sad to say that the end of my own marriage helped to get me the job, but it did. I hadn't planned on fighting him for anything after I found out about his affair, but once I found out that his mistress was pregnant I lost my mind. I wanted him to suffer in some way. I wanted him to feel what I felt when he took my dream from me. I had given up so much for him. When we decided to start trying for a family of our own, I stopped working. I gave up who I was and became the wife he wanted me to be. I took care of the house and the groceries, made dinner every night, and made sure I was always available to spend time—or have sex—with him. I don't necessarily blame him for that. I wanted to be a good wife to him. I wanted to make him happy, to be someone he was proud to have on his arm. I wanted him to know how much I appreciated him, which is why what he did killed me a little bit.

I didn't have any money of my own, and I knew I couldn't use a local firm to handle my divorce since so many of the lawyers in Boston were friends of Tom's. Then I happened upon a newspaper article about someone from my past: Abby Snider, a divorce attorney in New York City. I was three years older than she was, but we had been in the same group home. I looked after her as much as I could before she was adopted at age eleven by a well-off family in New York City. We lost contact after that, but she never forgot me—the same way I never forgot her. The story claimed that she was a righter of wrongs and a voice for the women she fought for. I needed a voice. I needed someone to fight for me, and Abby did. When I contacted her, she remembered me immediately and agreed to help me out.

Tom and his family were affluent, but it wasn't until I filed for divorce that I learned exactly how well Tom had done on his own. All I knew was that we were comfortable, we had a nice house in a beautiful neighborhood, we drove latest-model cars, and I didn't have to clip coupons. In the end, Tom didn't put up a fight. He gave me a little over $10 million in our divorce settlement without batting an eye. Maybe he felt guilty, but getting that settlement didn't make me feel any better. I would have rather had the life he promised me the day we got married.

The sound of the doorbell brings me out of my thoughts. As soon as I see the shadowy figure on the other side of the glass, I roll my eyes skyward and stomp across the highly polished dark hardwood floors.

"Yes?" I ask after I swing the heavy wooden door open.

"I figured you were busy packing, so I brought dinner," Tom says, holding up a brown paper bag between us like a peace offering.

I pull in a deep breath and watch him shift on his feet, looking uncomfortable. It's weird that I don't find him the least bit attractive now. When we got together I thought he was a good-looking man: he's tall and lean with blond hair and brown eyes that used to make me melt when he looked at me.

"Shouldn't you be home with your girlfriend and newborn?" I ask, not able to keep the bite out of my tone.

Since his daughter was born two months ago, he's been doing things like this more and more. That is, showing up unannounced, asking me to meet for dinner, calling all the time. Which is why I decided *not* to buy Tom out of the house, but to put it on the market and take the job Abby offered me instead. Living in the same city with him has been hard. I hate seeing him. I hated running into his pregnant girlfriend at the grocery store, where I had to endure her catty looks. I hate that his mom lives across the street and still thinks it's okay to stop by whenever she wants. Don't get me wrong, I love his mom, but seeing her is a reminder of the family I lost. I also really hate that Tom seems to think that he still has some kind of right to my time, that he can call or stop by whenever he feels like it.

"She's out," he says, and there is no ignoring the slight tic in his jaw. "Can I come in?"

"I'm busy, Tom. I have a lot to do before the movers get here in the morning."

He looks over my shoulder, into the house, before looking back to me. "I can help."

"I don't need any help," I state, blocking his way when he starts to take a step forward.

"Courtney, I . . ." His words trail off as he runs his fingers through his hair.

I used to find it endearing when he would do that as he tried to get his thoughts together, but now I just find it annoying. Really, I find everything about him annoying.

"Tom, just go home." I sigh, shaking my head.

"Can you cut me some slack here? Try to understand what I'm going through?"

"Cut *you* some slack?" I shake my head in disbelief. "I think I cut you too much slack, if you ask me. And what exactly are *you* going through?" I question snidely, not able to stop myself.

"My wife is leaving the state. I think I have a valid reason to be upset."

"Ex-wife." My jaw clenches as I spit out that reminder.

"I still love you."

"You got another woman pregnant while we were married. While I was going through fertility treatments. So I'm sorry, but I don't think you do love me. Really, I don't think you ever did." I'm tempted to shut the door in his face.

"You know I was going through a lot at work. With you trying to get pregnant . . . things weren't easy for me."

Inhaling sharply, I tighten my grip on the doorknob as I try to control the sudden fury that is coursing through my veins. "Screw. You."

I cannot *believe* I was married to this man. I can't believe that I didn't see him for the selfish asshole he is. I really must have been blind.

"Shit, I'm sorry." His eyes close briefly. "I didn't . . ." He shakes his head. "My head's all messed up. I want us to be friends. I miss you. I miss talking to you." Again with the talking. The last two years of our marriage, *I* did all the talking, and felt like I was losing my mind, like I was being unreasonable wanting time and attention from him.

"I *don't* want to be friends with you, Tom. Really, if I never saw you again it would be too soon."

"You don't mean that. You love me."

"Loved. I *loved* you. I don't love you anymore. I don't even like you."

"So this is it? You're moving to New York, and I'll never see you again?"

There is no denying the sadness in his voice, but I no longer care about his feelings.

"I wanted forever with you," I say quietly. "I wanted forever, and you took that from me. So yes, this is it. I don't want to be friends, and I don't want anything to do with you."

His eyes drop to his feet.

"You will never know how sorry I am," he tells me, meeting my gaze once more. He looks like he's really hurting, and my heart—which he already destroyed with his carelessness—crumples in my chest. I hate that he's in pain, but he didn't think about how I would be affected by what he was doing to me.

"Bye, Tom." I close the door on him and this chapter of my life.

~

"So what do you think?"

I'm looking around the house . . . Okay, maybe *house* is too loose a term, since the inside is completely bare. There's no kitchen or bathroom, actually; there aren't even walls. The structure is an outer shell that sort of kind of resembles a house.

"Ugh." I scan the room again, wondering if I'm missing something. John, my Realtor, laughs. John is a couple of years older than me. He's handsome in a Prince Harry sort of way, with copper-colored hair that makes his green eyes seem even brighter, a strong build, and an ever-present smile.

"I get it. It's not much to look at, but it's a great price. In this neighborhood, you won't find a deal like this again."

"It's over a million." I look around. "And there aren't even walls."

"Think of it as a blank canvas." He smiles, showing off a small dimple in his left cheek.

"I don't really have any other way to think of it, since there is nothing here." My lips start to twitch when he laughs again.

6

"I know a great interior architect. He's new to the city, but all of his work has been amazing. I'll set you up with him if you decide that this is the house for you."

"You really think this is a good investment?" I look around again.

"I showed you the comps for the neighborhood. Most of the houses on this street have been going for five million or more. I'm guessing that it will probably cost you eight hundred thousand or so to renovate. So yes, I really think this is a great investment."

Never in my life would I have thought that I would be talking about spending a million dollars on a home—or about so much for renovations. But here I am, standing in the empty shell of a house and thinking about doing just that. Just the thought of spending that kind of money makes me want to break out in hives, especially after a childhood during which my whole existence could fit into a carry-on suitcase.

"It's a cute neighborhood," I say out loud, more to myself than to John, as I walk over toward a window that overlooks a quiet street in Riverdale, a cute area in the Bronx.

"It's a really *nice* neighborhood. If you decide to have kids one day, the schools around here are some of the best in the city."

Kids. That dream is long gone. If I do get this place, I would get a dog—or maybe a few of them—to keep me company. "How long do I have to think about this?"

"I'd love to tell you to take all the time you need, but this place is going to go fast. The developer who bought it and started fixing it up wants it off his hands as quickly as possible, which is why it's priced like it is."

"So I need to make an offer," I say, turning around to face him. I feel anxiety rush through my stomach. I've never been good at making decisions without a lot of time and thought.

"If you're going to make an offer, I'd say do it sooner than later." He nods, shoving his hands into the pockets of his pressed slacks.

7

I turn and take in the empty space. I love the area, and I know he's right. Homes on this block are going for a lot more than I would be paying, even including renovations. It would be an investment, probably a good one. I need to start my life over, and part of doing that is making a home for myself.

"Okay," I agree.

His head tips to the side.

"I'll make an offer, but promise me that if it's accepted, you'll get me in touch with your guy as soon as possible."

I don't mind the place that I'm subletting, but spending close to five grand a month for rent makes me feel nauseated. Then again, there aren't too many places in the city in decent areas for less than that.

"You got it." He grins, showing off his bleached-white smile. "Now come on. I'll take you out to lunch." He closes the door to the house behind us as we step out onto the front stoop.

I look at my watch and shake my head. "I can't. I need to be across town."

"All right. I'll just get all the paperwork for the offer ready and email the documents you need to sign."

"Sounds good." I give his arm a squeeze before he sticks out his hand for a cab that pulls up a second later. "Do you think telling them I'll pay cash will speed up the process?" I ask as he opens the taxi door for me.

"It won't hurt," he says with a shrug. He's not even surprised at the idea of someone paying a million in cash for a house. Then again, as a Realtor in one of the most expensive cities in the world, he's probably used to it.

"I'll keep an eye out for your email." I smile as I slide into the back of the cab. Looking at the house as the car pulls away, I can feel my stomach fluttering with nervous excitement.

Chapter 2

JUST THE TWO OF US

LUCAS

"Daddy, I'm ready for you to come tuck me in and read me a story," Madeline says. My little girl is standing just outside her bedroom door, her dark hair still wet from her shower, with a sweet smile on her little face and wearing a pair of bright-pink pajamas with unicorns all over the cotton material.

"Did you brush your teeth?" I glance at the clock and see it's already eight.

"Yep." She smiles, and I narrow my eyes.

"Did you put all your girl stuff back on your shelf in the shower?" Her eyes light up, and a giggle escapes her lips. "Yes, Daddy."

"Thank goodness." I place my hand over my heart as she hops into bed, pulling the blankets over her lap. "I don't need another glitter accident like the one I had last week."

She falls back into bed, laughing hard.

Smiling at her, I can't help but laugh myself. It's funny now, but it wasn't funny last week when I accidentally used her body wash instead of my own, leaving a coating of glitter on my skin that seemed impossible to wash off. I went to work looking like that damn silver troll doll from that movie. Thank god I didn't have to meet with any clients that day and was able to hide out in my office.

"You're so silly, Daddy." She sits up with a smile on her face.

"So what book are we reading tonight?" I watch her turn on her lamp before I turn off the overhead light and head across the room to sit on the edge of her bed.

"This one." She hands me the book.

I look at the cover and smile. "Again?"

"It's my favorite." She scoots over, and I lie down next to her. I lift my arm so she can tuck her small body against my side like she has been doing since she was a newborn.

"All right." I open the book and start to read the story of the princess and the pea, stopping only once her soft snore fills my ears. Seeing that her eyes are closed, I place my lips against her smooth forehead and hold them there. I never thought that one day it would be just the two of us, that I would end up a single father. When I met Madeline's mother, Eva, I didn't really think much about the kind of woman she was—I got stuck on her looks and her entertainment value. I was a dick . . . or maybe I was just thinking with my dick when it came to her. She was beautiful, had a great smile, and could be funny in the right situation. We had off-the-charts chemistry, and, at the time, all of that was enough for me. But when she told me she was pregnant, everything changed.

I had grown up seeing my parents in love and making their marriage work. I had always wanted a family, and I thought I could make one with Eva if I tried hard enough. I asked her to marry me when she was two months pregnant. We got married the next month in a small ceremony at my family's church. For a while things were good—I won't lie and say they were great, because they never were, but they were good. We found a routine that worked for us, mostly involving me allowing her to do whatever she wanted to do.

When Madeline was born, Eva and I were both busy—I with work, she with taking care of our home and our new daughter when I wasn't around to help out. Over time things with Eva got more difficult. It became harder to pretend I was happy, and I found myself avoiding her. I didn't like the way she treated Madeline. I didn't like that she was more interested in hanging with her friends than being a mom. For a long time, I let shit go. If we divorced, I didn't want my daughter to grow up seeing me only on weekends or whenever the courts allowed me time. When Madeline turned five, though, I couldn't avoid the inevitable any longer. I couldn't even look at myself in the mirror without wondering who was looking back at me. I was miserable, lost, and living a lie with a woman I could hardly stand to be in the same room with.

When I made the decision to end our marriage, I half expected Eva to put up a fight, or to try to use Madeline against me to get whatever she wanted in the divorce. I soon found out that she already had a backup plan. She had been having an affair with a man who—lucky for me—didn't want to raise another man's child. Eva gave me full custody and moved in with the guy. She hasn't been around much since Madeline and I moved from Connecticut to the city for a fresh start almost two years ago. I hate that my baby is growing up without a mom, but part of me is thankful that she is growing up without *her* mom, a woman who chose a man over her child. Madeline does miss her mom—or the idea of her mom. I see it in her eyes when she talks about her friends' mothers or when something comes up that she should be sharing with a mom. Luckily, there are some really great women in our lives. My mother and my brothers' wives have stepped up to the plate and attempted to fill the void left by Eva.

"I love you, honey." I place one more kiss against her forehead before carefully scooting her off my chest. I get out of bed and tuck the blankets around her, then set down the book and shut off her lamp. I turn on her nightlight, which casts tiny stars on the ceiling, and leave her room. Tomorrow I have work and Maddi has school, so it's going to be an early morning of getting myself ready before getting her up, which is a process all its own.

Rubbing my eyes, I walk across the apartment to turn off the lights before shutting off the television and heading for bed. I strip out of my clothes, get in bed, pick up my cell, and make sure my alarm is set. I notice a message from my secretary, Sam, about a potential new client. I was worried about moving to New York City. The cost of an apartment alone was enough to give me heart palpitations, but it was the best thing I ever could have done. Impeccable Designs is one of the best architectural firms in the city, and word of mouth has brought me more business than I know what to do with. If things keep going like they have been, I should be able to get a bigger place for Madeline and me in the next year or so. I moved into Fawn's old place—my brother's wife—and although it's nice, it's small. Madeline's room isn't even really a room. I think it might have been a storage closet at one point. Still, I'm lucky that she has her own space. Honestly, I can't complain about our living situation, since Levi and Fawn live right across the hall and are always willing to help out with Madeline anytime I need it, like when I have to work late or when she gets sick at school and I'm unable to get away from the office to pick her up.

I plug in my cell, then drop it on the side table. I shut my eyes. Just like every night since I left Eva, I sleep easily and soundly—something I wasn't able to do for years.

Chapter 3

TROLLS

COURTNEY

Rushing across the street with the crowd before the light turns red, I stumble when one of my heels catches on a crack in the asphalt. Luckily, I right myself just before I do a face-plant. Unluckily, I hear a loud snap and feel my ankle wobble as the heel of my shoe breaks off.

"Crap." I don't stop, because the honking cars won't let me. Instead I hobble across the street to the sidewalk. Only then do I stop to look at the damage. Leaning with one hand against a light pole, I pull off my shoe and inspect it. For a shoe that cost close to a grand, the thing sure did break like it was cheap plastic. Then again, Tom did surprise me with them, so I shouldn't be shocked they are falling apart. With a sigh I look around, praying that there is a store nearby where I can run in for a new pair of shoes. Hell, I'd even take a pair of plastic flip-flops right now. Not seeing a place, I glance at my watch. I have about ten minutes to get to my meeting with the interior architect who's been working on the plans for my house. I haven't met Mr. Fremont yet. Until today I've mainly dealt with his secretary. He came so highly recommended that my hopes are high that he'll have something amazing for me. Especially since, in all honesty, I don't have the imagination to muster up even one idea of what I want.

Having no other choice, I put my shoe back on. There is no way in hell I'm walking on a dirty New York City street without it. More than a few strange looks are directed my way as I walk awkwardly down the sidewalk, but I try to ignore them and focus on not killing myself. As soon as I reach the office building where Impeccable Designs is located, I head through security and take the elevator up. When I make it to the forty-ninth floor, I take in the dark-gray walls hung with framed blueprints. I wobble past a small sitting area with two low leather chairs, a glass coffee table, and a black leather couch, and make my way up to the front desk, where a beautiful blonde woman is watching me with a look of concern on her pretty face.

"Can I help you?" she asks.

I carefully put all my weight on the heel that isn't broken.

"I have a meeting with Mr. Fremont."

She turns her head toward the computer and begins to type.

"Courtney Williams?" Her eyes come back to me, and I nod. "I'll let him know you're here. You can take a seat over there and wait. Do you need anything? A coffee or water?"

"Do you happen to have an extra pair of shoes?" I half joke, and she smiles sympathetically.

"I actually do." She fishes around under her desk, pulls out a small drawstring bag, and holds it out to me. "You can have these. I have an extra pair in the drawer."

"Are you serious?" I ask in disbelief, taking the pouch and opening it to find a pair of black, soft cotton flats with rubber soles.

"We girls gotta help each other out." She shrugs, but I want to jump across the desk and hug her.

"Thank you. I'll pay you back."

"Pay it forward," she says.

I blink at her. She looks like a model, and most of my experience with women who look like her has been that they only ever think of themselves. They just don't *do* things like help another woman out when she needs a pair of shoes or tell that woman to pay it forward instead of asking for her firstborn child. Okay, I should say *most* of the wives of Tom's colleagues were like that.

"Thank you." I make a mental note to send her the biggest bouquet of flowers I can order as I take off my heels and put on the flats, then tuck my broken shoes away in my purse.

"You're welcome." We exchange smiles, then I lift my head when my name is rumbled through the sparse but elegantly decorated space. When my gaze locks on the owner of the voice, my whole world tips. *Exquisite* is the word that comes to mind as I take in Mr. Lucas Fremont. He's wearing a black tie, stark-white dress shirt, and black slacks. His clothing fits his lean, muscular frame like a second skin. Moving my eyes to the rest of him, I can tell he's a man who knows he looks good but doesn't put a lot of effort into his appearance. His hair is a tad too long, dark blond with natural highlights. His skin is tan—but tanned by the sun, not a tanning bed, which seems to be popular with men nowadays. His jaw is square and not completely clean of scruff, like he might have forgotten to shave this morning. His eyes . . . his eyes are a light blue, and they seem to glow more for being framed by his dark lashes.

"Courtney." That deep rumble of his breaks me out of my perusal, and that's when I notice that he's moved closer. So close that I can see his eyes are not blue like I thought. They're more of a soft gray with a dark-blue ring around the irises.

"Uh. Yes." I swallow, take a step toward him, and hold out my hand in his direction.

"It's nice to meet you." The moment his fingers wrap around mine and our eyes lock, my tipped world tumbles sideways. Blinding heat courses through my veins, and all the oxygen in the room suddenly disappears, leaving me breathless. Never in my life have I ever had this kind of reaction to a man. Never has one touch left me so completely vulnerable.

What the hell is wrong with me? Maybe I ate something I shouldn't have. That has to be it.

"If you'll follow me." He lets go of my hand, and I bite my lip to keep from reaching for him again. I walk behind him down a brightly lit hall lined with framed photos of houses. When we reach his office, I walk in behind him, then stop as he shuts the door.

The click of the latch makes me jump. My eyes start to roam his body again. They catch on his tie—or, more accurately, a glittery troll sticker that's stuck to his tie.

Blinking, I tip my head back because he towers over me. I swallow nervously when our eyes connect before blurting, "Trolls."

"What?"

I pull my eyes from his and reach out, almost touching the sticker on his tie. "Trolls."

"My daughter." He pulls the tie away from his body and smiles while rubbing his thumb over the glittery sticker. "She thinks she's funny."

Daughter. My stomach drops in disappointment. Of course he's married with a daughter. A man who looks like he does *would* be married with a daughter. A daughter who probably looks just like her mother, with whom he's madly and obsessively in love.

"So . . . I think you have plans for me." My eyes widen. "I mean plans for me to look at."

"Yeah." His lips twitch like he's fighting back a smile. He clears his throat before he takes a step away from me. He walks toward the desk.

He even has a great walk.

I close my eyes for a moment when his back is to me, willing myself to pull it together and not make a fool out of myself. I make a mental note to figure out what I ate so I don't eat it again.

"John said you didn't know what you were looking for or what kind of design you were after, so I did a few mock-ups. If you see something that you think you or your husband might like, we can go from there." He turns to face me, bringing a laptop with him.

"I'm not married." I could swear his shoulders relax, but I know I must be seeing things.

"We can sit on the couch. That way you can see a little easier."

"Sure," I agree, following him to the simple gray couch and black coffee table that are situated catty-corner to his desk. Taking a seat close—but not too close—to him, I set my bag on the floor near my feet. "How old is your daughter?"

"She's six, almost seven," he says without looking up at me. "She's all girl and a complete handful, but I wouldn't change her for the world."

Sweet *and* hot. God, why oh why do all the men like him have to be taken?

"Is that her?" I ask, looking at a small red-framed photo on the desk that's across the room. It shows a little girl with dark hair like his. She's holding a butterfly in the palm of her hand, her eyes lit up and a smile of absolute wonder on her adorable little face.

"Yeah." His expression becomes so gentle that my heart melts. "That was from last summer, when I took her to the butterfly garden."

"She's adorable. You and your wife made a beautiful girl."

"I'm not married." His eyes meet mine, and the air between us shifts as our gazes lock once again.

"Oh."

His eyes drop to my mouth and seem to darken right before he suddenly turns the computer toward me.

"This is the first design."

My eyes widen in complete awe. On the screen is an image of the outside of the brick home I just purchased, but without the scaffolding that is there now. Under each window is a square black box full of colorful flowers, and the door to the house is painted a golden yellow that stands out against the dark-red brick. When he moves his finger across the screen, various images of the interior come up. The front entrance has bright light, with light wood floors and gray walls with white trim. The living room features a large fireplace surrounded by cozy-looking couches, and the kitchen has white cabinets, stainless-steel appliances, and a large island. On and on he clicks, through picture after picture, virtually walking me through all three thousand square feet. He ends in the master bedroom suite, which features large floor-to-ceiling windows and a master bath with an old-time claw-foot tub and pedestal sinks. I might not have known what I wanted my house to look like, but after seeing the home that he created, I know that it's *exactly* what I want. There isn't one thing I would change about his design.

"It's perfect." My voice fills with awe, and I lift my eyes to meet his.

"I know that there are some elements that are a little more rustic than most New Yorkers like, but you can change them out for a more modern look easily. I also have a few other plans drawn up that we can look at."

"I love everything. All of it. I didn't think it would be possible to see the house as anything more than it is right now, but what you did is magic. I love it, and I can't imagine changing anything. Really. I can't wait to see it when it's done."

"There's *nothing* you'd want to change?" he asks, studying me.

"Nothing." I shake my head, looking at the photo of the master bath once more. "I love it."

"You might be the easiest woman I've ever met." His eyes widen, and his cheeks are tinged with pink. "I mean . . ."

"It's okay." I let out an awkward giggle with a shake of my head. "I know what you mean. How long do you think all this will take?" I wave my hand down at the computer he's still holding between us.

"My guess is about eight months. It might be a little longer if the contractors find anything they need to fix before they start putting up walls."

"Eight months." I sigh in disappointment. I know logically that this kind of work is impossible to do overnight, but I still wish it could be. "I guess since Rome wasn't built in a day, I shouldn't think my house will be, either."

"It will all be worth it when it is done."

"You're right," I agree. Then I ask, "So what now?"

"You just need to sign off on these. I'll get in touch with the contractors and get them the plans. Once I have that done, we will go and pick out the appliances and finishes. I find that it's best if a client actually gets a chance to see and touch the things they are purchasing."

"Cool." I smile, trying not to get too excited at the prospect of seeing him again.

"So John said you're new to the city?"

"Yeah, I've been here about four months now," I say, watching him get up and return to his desk.

"Where did you live before?"

"Boston, just outside the city."

"What brought you here?" he asks, doing something on his computer that makes the printer next to it spit out papers rapidly.

"I got a job at a law firm in the city . . . and I needed a change."

"You're a lawyer?"

"No, I work as a paralegal."

He picks up a stack of papers from the tray on top of the printer. "I think John mentioned that you were new here as well?"

"Yeah. Well, I guess I'm still considered new, even though I've been here awhile now."

"Do you like it?"

"It's taken me time to get used to it, but I like it. It helps that my brother and his wife are here, so I have family close. What about you? Do you have any family around?"

"No, it's just me," I answer.

He nods, picking up a pen before coming back to take a seat next to me—right next to me—so close that his hard thigh rubs against mine through the light material of my wide-leg dress slacks. So close that I can smell the subtle scent of his cologne.

"These are the images we went over. I just need you to initial each page, along with the blueprint of the layout."

Taking the papers and the pen from him, I sit forward and rest the stack of papers on the coffee table to start initialing each page. It doesn't take me long to sign off on each one, but I can't take more time since it would look like I was stalling. Reminding myself that I just got divorced and that the man I had planned to spend the rest of my life with screwed me over in a big way, I start to sign more quickly. Once I'm finished I hand him back the stack of papers and pick up my purse.

"Thank you so much. I really love the work you did," I say, avoiding his eyes by looking at a space just above his ear. "I look forward to hearing from you."

I move to the door, and my breath hitches when I feel his heat at my back and his hand brushing my arm as he reaches past me for the doorknob.

"Does Sam have your number?"

I turn and look at him. "I believe so."

"Let me get it, just in case she doesn't."

I bite my lip as he pulls out his cell phone. I quickly give him my number, along with an awkward smile, before hurrying out of his office. I swear I can feel his eyes burning into my back.

"Did everything go okay?" the receptionist asks as I pass her desk.

"Great. Everything went great. Thank you again for the shoes."

"No problem. Have a good day." She smiles brightly, giving me a small wave.

"You too."

I rush for the elevator and press the call button. Thank god it doesn't take long to show up. When I'm inside and the doors close,

I take a breath for the first time. My heart is pounding hard against my rib cage like I have been running for miles. I *am* running—maybe not physically, but I am running away from Mr. Fremont. A handsome man whose eyes light up when he talks about his daughter. A guy whose cheeks get pink with embarrassment when he makes an awkward comment about me being easy. Yes, I'm totally running from a man like him, because at one time I believed that Tom was too good to be true—and I know exactly where that got me.

~

"How do you feel about everything so far?" Abby asks as I take a sip of wine during our dinner date. Abby is young for a lawyer, or at least young for a lawyer as successful as she is. Even though she's just a few years younger than my thirty-four, she looks twenty-five tops. Her dark hair is cut in a sophisticated bob, and she has a pixie-like baby face that works for her. The people she goes up against never see the pit bull coming.

"I feel good, really good. Free, actually," I say, watching her expression soften in understanding.

The day I called her about representing me, I never thought that our friendship would fall right back into place, but that's exactly what happened. Only now the roles have been reversed: she's been the one looking out for me.

"Good." She picks up her own glass, taking a sip. "Have you met anyone since you've been here? I have a couple of guys I'd like to introduce you to if not."

"I don't think I'm ready for that." I smile. "I don't know when I will be ready to date again. I *am* thinking about getting a dog to keep me company."

"What kind?" she asks, sitting forward and looking excited about the idea, probably because she has three dogs of her own.

21

"Something small that's okay with living in the place I have now."
I laugh.

Her nose scrunches up. She knows all about my sublet. "How are things going with the renovations?"

The muscles in my stomach clench. Since my meeting a week ago with Mr. Fremont—who has insisted I call him Lucas—he's texted me a couple of times with updates about the contractors and to set up a time next week to meet at an appliance warehouse in New Jersey to see a few of the things he's picked out.

"It's going, but it's going to be a long road."

"I can't wait to see it when it's done."

"Me too. I think I'll feel more settled once I get into the house and start making a home for myself here in the city."

"That's understandable," she says gently. "Have you heard from Tom?"

"He's called a few times, but I haven't answered. I don't want to speak to him. I've talked to his mom, though."

"How was that?" She knows all about my relationship with Tom's family, especially his mom.

Shrugging, I let out an audible sigh. "She's still disappointed that I left. She tried to convince me that if I just gave Tom a chance he would make things right." I take another sip of wine before continuing. "She's the only real mom that I have ever known, so it sucks that by ending my relationship with Tom, things between us have become strained."

"She probably understands that things aren't like they used to be," she says quietly.

I shrug once more, not sure she's right.

"I don't know. I know that she's torn, feeling like she has to choose between her son and me, but I also know that she will always take Tom's side. When I first found out about Tom's affair and went to her, she told me I should basically turn a blind eye to what her son was doing."

"Yeah, I remember." She rolls her eyes. "I know from firsthand experience that a lot of women just look the other way. It happens more than it should. But seriously, what woman *in the world* would be okay with her husband sleeping with another woman after promising himself to her and her alone?"

"Not me," I state adamantly.

"Me neither, honey." She raises her glass and so do I. We clink them together. "I know that I shouldn't say this out loud, but if I found out what you found out . . . I would be doing a lot more than taking money from my husband. I would be taking his manhood, bronzing it, and hanging it from my rearview mirror as a trophy and a warning to any man who ever thought of wronging me again."

Laughing at the visual, I shake my head. "There have to be a few good men out there, right?"

"God, I hope so. I'm extremely wary when it comes to the opposite sex after seeing the things I've seen and hearing the things I've heard in my line of work."

"I don't know if I could ever trust another man again," I admit sadly.

I don't know if I could ever believe another man who told me that I was all he wanted.

"I don't blame you. But, like my mom is always telling me, if you dig in the dirt deep enough, you will always end up finding something worth treasuring."

"I don't think I will be digging anytime soon," I say, ignoring the image of Lucas that pops into my head. An image that has popped in a lot since we met.

"Well then, here's to being single in the city." She grins, and we clink our glasses once more, laughing this time.

Chapter 4

STEPPING IN

LUCAS

As soon as I reach the warehouse in New Jersey, I head toward the front entrance. I shouldn't be looking forward to this meeting as much as I am, but there is no denying that I've been counting down the days over the last week.

I step inside the entryway, and my eyes zero in on Courtney immediately. I fight back a groan when I see what she has on. The last time I saw her she was wearing black dress pants that molded to her ass and a sheer top with a lace cami underneath that peeked through when she bent over. I thought *that* outfit was sexy, but today's black dress, which is wrapped tightly around her body, accentuating her full breasts, small waist, wide hips, and long legs, might be the sexiest thing I have ever seen a woman wear—in *or* out of the bedroom. The only thing I would change is her hair. Today it's up in a tight bun that exposes her delicate neck and soft face. I like her hair down; it reaches almost to her waist, and it looks so soft that my fingers itch to touch it, to wrap my hands in it as I kiss her, to feel it against my chest as she rides me or to see it spread out over my pillow as she sleeps.

As I walk over to her, I try not to puff out my chest when I see her checking me out the same way I was just checking her out. "I hope you haven't been waiting long."

"I just got here." She smiles.

Her breath hitches when I wrap my hand around her upper arm and touch my lips to her soft cheek, getting a hint of the soft floral scent she's wearing.

"Good." I lean back, then wrap my fingers around her elbow so I can lead her into the showroom. "How have you been? How's work?"

"I've been good. Work's work. There is always some kind of excitement happening, but then again, with the cases Abby takes on, it's not surprising."

I drop my eyes down to hers, liking a fuck of a lot that even when she's in heels I have to look down at her. "Abby's your boss?"

"Yeah."

"What kind of lawyer is she?"

"She's a divorce attorney, hence the constant excitement."

"I bet," I mutter.

Luckily, I didn't have to fight Eva for anything in our divorce, but I have no doubt that if she hadn't had another man waiting in the wings, things would have been ugly and drawn out.

"How have you been? How's your daughter?" she asks, the second part of her question coming out soft.

"Been good, and Madeline is good. One of her classmates is having a sleepover birthday party Saturday, and she's never been to one before so she's looking forward to it."

"That does sound like fun."

"Fun for her and her friends, yeah. I'm guessing that it's not going to be much fun for her friend's parents, since they are going to have ten six-year-old girls in their house causing chaos."

I smile as she starts to laugh.

I lead her toward the hardwood floors and pull out the sample that I've chosen for her house. "This is prettier in person than the image you saw on the computer."

She runs her fingers over the rough wood. "I love that it's not dark. My last house had dark wood, and you could see every speck of dust. I won't have to worry about constantly cleaning so people don't think I'm a slob when they see dog hair."

"You have dogs?"

"Not yet. I want at least one, possibly more," she tells me as she hands me back the piece of flooring.

"What kind of dog are you getting?"

"I don't know." Her brows draw together, and all I can think about is how cute she is. "Do you like dogs?"

"I grew up with them. My mom had a yorkie that used to yap all the time." I smile. "Once my brothers and I were old enough to take care of a dog, we got a hound mix named Sherlock."

"I've never had a dog before," she tells me as we walk toward the appliance section of the warehouse. "I don't even know if they are a lot of work."

"Dogs are easy; cats are easier," I tell her.

She tips her head to the side. "Maybe I should get a cat, then," she says, looking thoughtful. I throw my head back and laugh loudly, then stop when she touches my arm softly.

"You have a great laugh."

"Thanks." I clear my throat and wonder what the hell is going on in my head. The smallest touch from her sends my mind racing with a million dirty thoughts. "So this is your fridge." I point out the top-of-the-line refrigerator; it includes a display screen.

"This is cool." She touches the screen, then examines the price tag taped to the front. "I'm not sure that I need it, though." She turns to face me. "Do you have anything else in mind that doesn't cost so much?"

I'm honestly a little taken aback by her question. Most of my clients want the best of the best, regardless of cost. I know from her overall budget that she can afford this fridge—hell, she could probably afford one that's cast in gold. Her being conscientious of what she's spending makes me even more curious about her.

"There's a lot to choose from. We can look around. If you see something you like, I'll just take down the information and change it out."

"Perfect," she agrees.

The rest of our time at the warehouse goes pretty much the same: I show her the things I picked out; she picks out items that cost a little less. Before I'm ready, our time is up and we are leaving.

"Do you have a ride?" I ask once we're outside.

"I was just going to call a cab," she tells me, pulling out her cell phone. Wanting to spend even a few more minutes with her, I cover her phone and hand with mine.

"We can ride back together, maybe get lunch once we reach the city?" I suggest.

She studies me for what feels like forever, and a million emotions seem to play behind her gaze.

"Yeah, okay. Lunch sounds good," she finally agrees. "Let me just call my boss to let her know."

Five minutes later, we are both getting into the back seat of a cab. My cell rings just as we are heading over the George Washington Bridge. It's Madeline's school.

"Hello?"

"Mr. Fremont? This is Jane, the nurse at Ark Elementary School."

"Is Maddi okay?" I ask before she can say more.

"She threw up in class. I just took her temperature, and it's a hundred and two. She's resting, but she should really be at home. Someone needs to pick her up."

"Shit. I'm on my way. I should be there in"—I look around to see where we are—"about twenty minutes, tops."

"Take your time. She's lying down now," she tells me, but that does nothing to ease the worry in the pit of my stomach.

"Tell her I'm on my way," I say, ending the call.

"Is everything okay?" Courtney asks, worry etched into the skin around her eyes.

"Madeline got sick in class and has a temperature. Sorry, but I'm going to have to drop you off and then go to her."

"Don't worry about me." She shakes her head, then asks, "Where is her school?"

After I tell her, she leans forward and directs the driver to go there. Then she looks at me once more. "I'll just get on the train once we get there."

"Thank you." I let out a long breath.

"No problem. I really hope she's okay. Was she sick this morning?"

"No, she seemed fine." Guilt hits me hard as I wonder if I missed something.

"I'm sure she will be all right." Her hand covers and squeezes mine, which is resting on my thigh. "I think I heard on the news that there is a stomach bug going around. She probably just caught it."

"Yeah," I agree, not liking that my baby isn't feeling good and I'm so far away.

When we reach the school, I check in and then head to the nurse's office. I don't even bat an eye when Courtney comes in with me. As soon as I walk through the door, I see Madeline asleep on a small cot tucked against the wall. A blanket is pulled up to her shoulders.

"Mr. Fremont?" I nod as the nurse walks toward me. "I took her temp about five minutes ago, and it's down to a hundred and one, but you will probably want to give her some Tylenol once you get her home."

"I'll do that." I thank her before going to my baby and getting down on my haunches. I run my fingers over the top of her head, and she turns toward my touch before her eyes blink open.

"Daddy . . . ," she says, sounding tired. Her eyes slide closed.

"I'm here, baby." I carefully scoop her up in my arms. "Let's get you home."

"I don't feel good."

"I know you don't." I kiss her head and turn with her in my arms. I watch the nurse give Courtney Madeline's pink-and-purple polka dot backpack and a white piece of paper.

"Feel better, Madeline," Nurse Jane says as Madeline tucks her face against my chest.

Holding her, I walk out and stop on the sidewalk. Without a word Courtney puts out a hand for a cab; when it stops, she opens the door for me.

"Thank you."

"No problem. I . . . Do you need anything? Do you have stuff for her at your house?" I realize that I don't have anything at our place, that the Tylenol I do have has probably expired. She must see exactly what I'm thinking, because she grabs my arm and pushes me into the cab before getting in with us. "I'll ride with you, help you inside, then run to the store and get what you need so that you can stay with her."

"Thank you." My whole chest tightens. I'm touched by her concern and grateful that she's willing to help me out when we hardly know each other.

"No problem." Her eyes drop to Madeline, who's now asleep in my arms. There is no denying the longing in her eyes as she looks at my girl.

It's on the tip of my tongue to ask why she doesn't have kids, but it doesn't feel like the right time. I give the cab driver my address, then sit with my girl in my arms as we head the few blocks to our place. When we pull up outside, Courtney pays the driver and gets out, holding the door for me. "What's the code?" she asks when we reach the door to our building.

"Two-seven-one-nine," I tell her. After she punches it in, she follows me upstairs to our apartment.

"Where's your key?"

"Pocket." Her cheeks darken, and she bites her bottom lip.

Biting back a smile I shouldn't even have on my face, I lean to the side so she can reach into my pocket for the key. Once she has it, she ducks her head. I still glimpse the blush rising in her cheeks as she opens the door for us to go in.

"Let me put her down," I say softly, and she nods.

I walk across the apartment to Madeline's room and lay her down on her bed. Her forehead's not as warm as when I first got to her, so I sigh in relief. I kiss the top of her head, take off her shoes, change her out of her clothes into a nightgown, and tuck her in. Once I return to the living room, I see that Courtney is still standing near the front door, not looking around, not making herself at home, just standing there holding Madeline's bag.

"Do you just need Tylenol, or . . . ?"

"Tylenol, ginger ale, and some soup and crackers, if you don't mind stopping at the grocery store."

"I don't mind." Once I take the bag from her, I pull out my wallet.

"I have money," she says, watching me pull out a couple of twenties.

"I really appreciate this." I ignore her comment and place the cash in her hand.

"It's not a big deal." She looks away.

Without thinking, I wrap my fingers around her chin. Her head jerks toward me.

"It's a very big deal," I say.

She swallows. I let her go so I don't do what I *want* to do, which is to place my mouth on hers. Her eyes stay locked with mine, though, and something moves behind them that makes the urge to kiss her stronger.

"I'll be back," she quickly says before leaving.

I stare at the closed door for a long moment before shutting my eyes and tipping my head back. There *is* something between us. I feel it whenever I'm near her. I also know that something happened to her, something that has left her vulnerable. My gut tightens at the thought of someone hurting her, of *me* hurting her without even trying or knowing what I'm up against.

"Fuck." I run my fingers through my hair, then drop my hands and call the doctor to make sure I don't need to bring Maddi in before I go to check on her again.

~

"Jesus, did you buy out the store?"

Courtney is carrying at least ten bags when she returns.

"I talked to the pharmacist, and she told me what I should get for a six-year-old with a stomach bug."

I quickly help her with the bags and drop them on the counter. I look at them, then her. I raise a brow because she bought a lot more than just stuff for a stomach bug. Her shoulders jerk up, and then her nose scrunches adorably.

"I also didn't know what kind of soup she liked, so I got a few different kinds."

I pull out a stack of coloring books and magazines, then raise my brow again.

"I also thought that maybe she likes to color or read?"

"She's six." I glance at the *People* magazine on top of the pile and fight back a smile. And the urge to touch her again.

"Well . . ." She presses her lips together, then looks to the side like she's embarrassed. "Maybe she wants to keep updated on what's going on in Hollywood."

"Yeah." I can't control it any longer. She's just too cute. I chuckle, and she bites her bottom lip, making me fight back a groan.

Fuck, I really want to kiss her.

"Well, I should probably go. Will you let me know if she's okay?"

Go? She wants to go already? I search for something to make her stay.

"You bought enough soup to feed an army. It's only right that you stick around to help me eat some of it." Courtney looks unsure, so I continue. "I'll also make grilled cheese. I'm the master of grilled cheese." I put on what I hope is a charming-but-reassuring smile.

"Are you sure?" She looks toward Madeline's room.

"I'm going to give her some meds. She'll probably sleep for a while."

"I . . . Okay," she agrees.

My body relaxes. I dig through the bags and find the Tylenol. "Make yourself comfortable. I'll be just a few minutes."

I head to Maddi's room. I checked her temp after Courtney left earlier, and it was 100.2—high but not too high. Still, I know the medicine will help. I wake Maddi enough for her to take a dose and then wait until she's sleeping again before I leave her room. I leave her door cracked so I can hear her if she gets sick or wakes up. Then I head toward the kitchen area, taking off my tie and rolling up my shirtsleeves as I walk.

Courtney is in the kitchen, unbagging the items she picked up, when I make it around the peninsula that separates the kitchen from the living room.

"I think I might have gone overboard," she says, looking at the ten cans of soup stacked on the counter. Seeing the look on her face, I start to laugh again. "In my defense, I really didn't know what to get."

I laugh harder, and she starts to laugh with me.

"It's fine. Maddi loves soup. Plus, I think canned goods have a long shelf life, so they will keep for a while."

"Right . . . ," she mumbles.

I smile. I pull out the cheese and mayo for the grilled cheese from the fridge and grab a loaf of bread from the counter.

"Mayo?" she asks incredulously.

I answer without stopping what I'm doing. "Have you had grilled cheese with mayo?"

"Um . . . no. I didn't even know that was a thing."

"My mom always used mayo instead of butter. It makes the bread more crisp and adds a little flavor."

"Hmm." I can tell by the look on her face that she's not convinced.

"Trust me. You're going to love it," I say, then look at her feet when I see her shift in her heels. "Take off your shoes, baby."

Her eyes meet mine when I say the word *baby*. Her expression changes, and something sweet fills her eyes. "I . . ."

"Floors are clean. Take off your heels."

"All right."

I watch her ass as she walks to the edge of the kitchen and kicks off her heels.

When she comes back, I realize how much shorter she is without the added height. "How tall are you?"

"Around five one." She tilts her head to the side. "Why?"

"You're tiny," I state. She *is* tiny, compared to me.

Laughing, she shakes her head. "I think you're the only man who's ever called me tiny."

"You are tiny. I'm six two, more than a foot taller than you."

"I'm also a size fourteen. I'm not small by today's standards."

My eyes drift down her frame. I look into her eyes. "You're perfect." And she is. There is nothing more beautiful than a woman who looks like a woman, with curves and a softness that you can explore with your hands and mouth, then sink into without worry of getting cut on protruding bones and sharp edges.

"Thanks." Her cheeks once again get pink, and she looks away.

Smiling to myself, I get out a frying pan and small saucepan and set them both on the stove. Then I open a can of tomato soup and dump it into the pot before adding cream to it.

"What can I do to help?"

"Nothing. Just relax." I turn up the burners on the stove, then move to the fridge.

"We have apple juice, Sunny Delight, and Kool-Aid. What's your poison?" I look at her over the top of the open fridge door.

"What kind of Kool-Aid?"

"Cherry."

"I'll have a glass of that."

Her answer intrigues me once again. Courtney is all class, from the tips of her red-painted nails to the matching polish on her painted toes. I can't imagine her ever drinking Kool-Aid—at least not willingly.

"You got it." I grab a glass from the cupboard and fill it before handing it to her. She takes a sip, then her eyes close in what looks like bliss. "Good?"

"Yeah." She opens her eyes, and they meet mine. "I haven't had Kool-Aid in years, but it's still as good as I remember. Maybe even better now."

"Good." I smile at her, and she smiles back before I return to the stove.

"You didn't lie," Courtney says after I've finished making our plates and we are both sitting down at the island eating.

I glance over at her with my half-eaten sandwich in hand.

"This is the best grilled cheese I have ever eaten in my life."

"If you think *that's* good, you should try my Hamburger Helper. It's life-changing." She laughs, picking up her half-full glass of Kool-Aid. "Can you cook?"

"I can. Well . . . kind of."

"Kind of?" I raise a brow in question.

"I can follow a recipe."

"My mom taught me and my brothers how to cook. She used to say that her boys would know their way around a kitchen so that when we got married we wouldn't put all the cooking on our wives."

"Smart lady."

"The smartest."

"How many brothers do you have?"

"Three. Two live in Connecticut with their wives and kids, and my brother Levi and his wife, Fawn, live across the hall."

"And your parents?"

"They still live in Connecticut, in the house I grew up in. What about your family?"

All of a sudden, she looks away. I don't think she's going to answer, but when she does it's in a voice that makes my chest hurt.

"I grew up in foster care. I don't know who my parents are, and I don't have any siblings—or I don't know if I do or not."

"I'm sorry, baby." I touch her knee, and she nods without looking up at me. I try to imagine Courtney as a little girl growing up without the support only a family can give. My heart aches for her. I can't even begin to understand what that must have been like for a child.

"It's okay. It's my life, and part of my story."

"Yeah, still, I'm sorry."

"Thanks." Her eyes meet mine.

"Daddy!" Maddi calls.

I find her standing outside her bedroom door, rubbing her eyes. I lift her up off the ground. "You okay, honey?"

"Who's she?" she asks quietly, pointing at Courtney.

"My friend Courtney. She helped me get you home." I kiss the side of her head, noting that it now feels completely cool against my lips.

"She's pretty," she whispers.

I grin at my baby girl. "She is," I agree, carrying her across the room. "Courtney, I'd like you to meet Madeline. Madeline, this is Courtney."

Courtney comes over to us. "It's so nice to meet you, Madeline."

"You too," Maddi says softly, tucking her small body closer to mine.

"Are you feeling better?" Courtney asks her, starting to reach out to touch her but pulling back before she makes contact. Maddi nods. "Are you hungry?"

"Not really."

"Is your tummy still bothering you?"

Maddi's eyes come to me before she looks at Courtney, shaking her head no.

"I got you some popsicles."

"Popsicles?"

"Yeah, special ones," she says.

I remember shoving a box of Pedialyte pops into the freezer.

"Okay," Maddi says. Then she turns to look up at me. "I don't have to miss the party, do I, Daddy?"

"I don't know, honey. I think we need to wait and see how you feel over the next couple of days."

"Oh man." She drops her head back dramatically before lifting it again. "I *promise* I feel better already."

"I'm sure you do, honey, but we still need to see how you feel in a couple days."

She sighs like she's sixteen instead of six, and then her eyes get big. Even anticipating what's about to happen, I'm still not able to move fast enough.

She leans forward and pukes down the front of Courtney's dress.

"Oh, sweetie," Courtney whispers, looking worried. She pulls Maddi's hair away from her face as she continues to gag, then looks up at me with concerned eyes. "Maybe you should put her in the shower while I clean this up."

I nod, then carry my baby to the shower. I help her out of her nightgown and hand her a toothbrush while we wait until the water's warm. I place my hand against her forehead to make sure it's still cool, then I put her under the spray.

"I'm sorry, Daddy," she whimpers.

My gut tightens with worry. "It's okay, honey." I wash her hair, then get her out, wrap her in a towel, and carry her back to her bedroom. "Let's get you dressed and back into bed."

She nods, looking tired.

Once she's tucked back in, I sit on the side of her bed and caress her cheek. I run my hand over the top of her head. There is really no worse feeling than when your kid is sick and you're completely helpless to do anything about it but let the illness run its course.

"Is she okay?" At Courtney's quietly spoken question, I look toward the door.

"Yeah."

"Is she sleeping?"

"Yeah." I rub my hands over my face, then stand.

"Maybe you should take her to the doctor," she says as I step out of the room.

"I called her doc when you were at the store. She said the same thing you said earlier. There is a bug going around, and there is nothing she can do for her unless she gets dehydrated. She said just to let her rest and make sure she keeps drinking."

"Poor girl." She looks over my shoulder toward Maddi's bed. When I look at the mess on her dress, I cringe.

"Let me get you something to wear."

"That's not necessary. I'll go home and change."

"Courtney, she puked on you. I'm not letting you leave like that." I take her hand and lead her toward my bedroom, letting it go only when I open the top drawer of my dresser, where I keep my T-shirts. I hand her one, then open another drawer and give her a pair of my sleep pants. "You can use the shower." I nod toward the bathroom door. "Clean towels are on the shelf behind the door. Use whatever you want in there."

Before she can open her mouth to tell me no, I leave my bedroom and close the door behind me. I try—I *really* try—not to think about her naked in my shower, but I still think about her naked in my shower as soon as the water turns on. So I don't get a hard-on from the images that keep flashing through my mind, I keep myself busy with cleaning up the dishes and putting away shit that's been left out over the last couple of days. When Courtney comes out of my bedroom wearing my clothes, something in me shifts in a profound way. Everything becomes glaringly clear. I want her, and there is something between us—something huge. I haven't felt this kind of attraction to a woman *ever*. I've never wanted to know everything about a woman, from the big stuff to the little details.

"Thank you for letting me use your shower." She carries her wadded-up dress toward the island and tucks it inside her bag before turning to me. "I should go."

"You gonna be able to get home okay?"

"Yeah, I'll get a cab." She smiles, and I find myself walking toward her.

"Have dinner with me."

"I—" Her brows draw together, and she looks toward Maddi's door.

"Not tonight," I say, cutting her off. "Once Maddi's better. Have dinner with me."

"I don't know . . ."

"Just dinner. Casual, as friends." I know those last two words are a lie, but I don't feel bad about it. I will gladly lie through my teeth to get her to take a chance on me.

"Okay. Sure," she agrees. "And if you need anything at all, let me know. My place isn't far from here, so if you need help, I can be over pretty quickly."

"Thanks. And thanks again for all your help." I shove my hands in the front pockets of my slacks so I don't grab her like I want to.

"It wasn't a big deal."

"It was."

"I just did what anyone else would have done." She has no idea how untrue that is. While Eva and I were married, she would take off to hang out with her friends whenever Maddi was sick, saying she couldn't deal because then she'd get sick herself. It used to piss me the fuck off but, like everything else, I ignored it so there wouldn't be a fight.

I don't tell Courtney any of that, though. Instead, I move closer to her. "Text when you get home so I know you made it safe."

"I'm only about a five-minute cab ride. I'll be okay."

"Text when you get home," I repeat.

Her eyes flare with what looks like surprise and appreciation before she nods and picks up her purse, sliding it over her shoulder and then slipping on her heels.

I walk her to the door, then lean down and touch my lips to her cheek before I open it for her. "Have a good night, Courtney."

"You too, Lucas," she whispers right before she walks away.

I watch until she's out of sight before closing the door. I lean my forehead against the frame, really hoping that my gut is right about this woman and that she really is as sweet and perfect as I think she is.

Chapter 5

Taking Care of You

Courtney

My stomach turns, and I close my eyes, praying the nausea that's been plaguing me for most of the day will end soon. It's been three days since I helped Lucas with his daughter. Until today I've felt great—better than great. I have been secretly living on cloud nine and walking on air at the idea of seeing Lucas again.

I know it's too soon to be thinking about spending time with another man, but I want to get to know him. I also want to see him with Madeline again. I don't think I have ever seen a man so devoted to his child. Watching them together is beautiful. The evening I left his place, I texted when I got home as he'd asked me to. Since then, we've shared a few messages. Mostly him updating me about Madeline, who was feeling better the next day, which gives me hope for myself.

I pull my blankets up around my chin and shiver. I woke up this morning feeling a little off, but I didn't think much about it until I threw up the first time. Now I know feeling "off" was my body's way of warning me that I was coming down with something. Luckily, it's Saturday, so I don't have to worry about calling in to work and letting Abby down. Still, there are a million things I would have liked to get done today. My cell phone beeps with a message, and it takes all my energy to lift my arm out from under my blankets and grab it. When I see I have a text, I swipe my finger across the screen and sigh in disappointment as I read the message from Lucas.

Wanted to see if you're up to dinner tonight with me? Maddi's feeling better but planning on hanging with my sister-in-law and watching movies since she's not allowed to go to her friend's birthday party.

Darn. I'd really love to see him.

Sorry, I think I caught Madeline's bug ... Another night?

I press "Send" and have started to close my eyes when my phone rings. I don't look at who's calling, I just swipe and put the phone to my ear.

"Hello?"

"You're sick?" Lucas's deep voice asks.

My stomach, which was already feeling funny, feels funnier.

"Yeah."

"Do you have meds? What's your address?" He asks the second question before I can even open my mouth to answer his first one.

"Why?" I ask as a wave of nausea hits me hard.

"What's your address?" he repeats. I give it to him without thinking, because my stomach rolls and bile crawls up the back of my throat. I drop my cell so I can cover my mouth with my hand, then toss back the blankets and rush to the toilet, where I puke again.

With my eyes closed and my body still heaving, I lift my head from the arm that's resting on the edge of the toilet and turn on the shower. Once it's warm, I get in and lean against the cold tile. I don't think I have ever been this sick before. With the little energy I have left, I wash up, then brush my teeth. I make it back to my bedroom in a towel and get under my blankets. I don't remember falling asleep, but the next thing I know I'm awakened by someone knocking on my door. I try to ignore them, but the knocking doesn't stop—and soon turns to pounding.

"What the heck?" I groan out loud as I toss back the blankets and get out of bed, tucking my towel around me as I head across my apartment. I open the door a crack and peek through.

"Lucas?" I blink up at Lucas's handsome face, wondering if I'm imagining him standing in my doorway. "What are you doing here?"

"I'm here to take care of you." He gently pushes the door open, then steps inside.

My eyes follow him as he walks through my apartment and into the kitchen. He's carrying three fabric bags. It takes more than a few seconds for my brain to catch up and for me to get out a "What?"

He drops the bags on the counter, then comes back toward me and takes the still-open door from my grasp, shutting it. "I'm here to take care of you." His eyes meet mine before slowly moving down my body. "Maybe you should go get something on. You're sick and should be dressed warmly."

My mouth opens and closes with a hundred questions before I can get out one word again. "What?"

"Get something on, baby." He takes my elbow and propels me toward my bedroom.

I know I should feel at least a little bit awkward that I'm only in a towel, but I honestly don't have the energy. I *definitely* don't have the energy to put my foot down and demand an explanation for his showing up at my place and saying he's here to take care of me.

"Where is Madeline?"

"With my brother and his wife. They got a pizza and are hanging out, watching a movie."

"Oh." I think I remember him texting me that.

"Have you eaten?" He stops at my bedroom door.

My stomach recoils at the idea of putting anything inside it.

"All right, no food," he says softly, reading my expression. "But you should try to drink something. Get dressed. I'll make you some peppermint tea. That'll help with the nausea."

He pulls the door closed, and I stare at it for a long time, trying to figure out why my chest feels so heavy and why my nose is stinging like I'm about to cry. It takes me a few minutes to realize it's because Tom *never* took care of me when I was sick. Even when I was going through round after round of fertility treatments, he didn't take care of me. He didn't hold my hand when I had to give myself a shot. He didn't tell me everything would be okay when I cried my eyes out because of the stress and the hormones they were putting into my body. Not once in all the years we were together did he ever offer to take care of me.

"You are not going to cry," I tell myself as I pull in a deep breath through my nose to fight back the tears filling my eyes. Then I pull in another one, and another. Only once I know I'm okay do I get dressed.

I pull on a pair of light-pink, wide-leg sleep pants with tiny purple flowers on them and a matching tank. I put on a long sweater. I pull up my hair in a messy bun, then open the door to my bedroom. I spot Lucas in the kitchen, emptying the shopping bags he brought with him. His eyes find me and soften around the edges.

"I didn't buy a hundred different kinds of soup," he informs me as I enter the room. "But I did get a few different movies since I wasn't sure what you're into."

"This is really nice, but—"

"Here." He cuts me off, holding a mug out toward me.

I take it and feel the warmth from it seep through to my cold fingertips.

"Just small sips," he instructs.

I nod, studying him. He looks different today, with stubble covering his jaw, a plain black T-shirt that's stretched across his broad chest, jeans that are faded in all the best spots, and sneakers that have seen better days.

"You look different," I blurt like a total dweeb.

He grins. "I haven't had to go into the office in a few days, so I haven't had a reason to shave." He rubs his hand over his cheek, and my fingers itch to do the same thing. "Come on." He picks up the stack of movies sitting on the counter, then takes my elbow again and leads me to the couch. "I'll put in a movie."

"I'm probably going to just fall asleep," I admit when he drops my elbow so I can take a seat on the couch.

"I don't mind." He picks up the remote, and I watch in fascination as he sets up the movie.

I haven't even figured out how to use the full system yet. Tucking my feet under me, I sip the tea, then frown when he disappears behind me into my bedroom. When he comes out a second later, he hands me my blanket and pillow. I'm touched.

"Get comfortable," he says before heading into the kitchen. I hear the microwave go on, and shuffling noises as he moves around.

I arrange my pillow on the armrest, set down my cup on the coffee table, and then cover myself with the blanket. I smile at the movie he chose. I love a good suspense flick. I haven't yet seen *Gone Girl*, but I did read the book and enjoyed it.

"I've been meaning to watch this," I tell him when he takes a seat on the other end of the couch, near my feet.

"Me too, but I'm thinking it probably won't be as good as the book."

"You read the book?" There is no hiding the surprise in my tone.

"I read all the time." He shrugs, catching me off guard.

"What kinds of books do you like?"

"Mostly mysteries." He shrugs one shoulder. "But I'll read fantasy if the mood strikes."

"So you read for enjoyment?"

He nods, and I sigh. Add another line item to the ever-growing list of things I like about him. I have always loved to read. Growing up, I didn't always have access to a TV, but I did always have a library card. When I was with Tom I stopped reading for a while, because I was so caught up in our life together. Tom only read what he had to read for work, so I didn't think about it. Two years before our marriage ended, I got a Kindle and started reading again. Looking back, I realize that I was reading to escape the reality of our deteriorating marriage. It was easier to be focused on a fictional couple's relationship than my own.

"Why do you seem so surprised?" Lucas's words bring me out of my thoughts.

"I don't know. I guess I'm just surprised that you like reading. I don't know many men who read for fun."

"Shouldn't judge a book by its cover." He grins, and I grin back while rolling my eyes. He lifts a fork with what looks like chicken and broccoli on the end of it to his mouth and takes a bite.

"What is that?"

"Grilled chicken and vegetables. Are you hungry now?"

"I'm not ready for food," I say.

His expression softens with sympathy before he reaches out and rubs the top of my foot, which is tucked against his hard thigh.

"Just rest."

"You know, I'm starting to realize that you're a little bossy."

"Rest."

"I *am* resting." I point out the obvious.

"Good. Then keep doing it." He smiles and takes another bite from the container he's holding. I debate whether to add bossiness to the "things I like about him" list. I'm not exactly sure if it's a good thing or not. Instead of focusing on him and the fact that he's in my apartment because he came to take care of me, I turn my attention to the movie—which is really good but still isn't as good as the book. I've come to find that no movie is ever as good as the book it's based on. When it finally comes to an end, I expect Lucas to tell me he's going to leave, but he doesn't. He puts in another movie. This one is a comedy that I mostly doze through, even though I hear him laugh every now and then before I fall asleep.

I feel myself being jostled, and my eyes flutter open. It takes me a moment to realize I'm being lifted off the couch.

"Lucas . . . ," I whisper, wrapping one arm around his shoulder to hang on.

"Putting you to bed, locking up, and heading home," he says, carrying me across the room.

"I can walk." I try to wiggle out of his grasp, but his hold on me tightens.

"I like carrying you." He kisses my forehead, then lays me in my bed.

The spot where his lips touched me tingles. I try to focus on his face in the dark. "Thank you for coming over. Sorry I was kind of lame."

"I like spending time with you, and you're *not* lame." He sits on the side of my bed and places his hands on the bed on opposite sides of my hips, caging me in. "I'll be over tomorrow after I get Maddi settled with my brother."

"You don't need to do that."

"I know, but I still will."

He leans forward, and I swear he's going to kiss me. I wait for it, my heart beating hard, but instead I feel his lips against the tip of my nose. "Sleep good, baby."

"Thanks," I whisper.

I watch him disappear out my bedroom door only to come back a moment later with my pillow and blanket. After he tucks me in, he leaves again.

I hold my breath until I hear the front door close.

Before I fall back asleep, I try to remind myself that it's way too soon for me to be thinking about starting a relationship with another man. But there is no denying that I really want to get to know Lucas Fremont—a guy whose cheeks turn pink when he says something that could be misconstrued, a guy who talks about his daughter with a softness in his eyes that is beautiful, a guy who takes care of his baby girl like there is nothing else that he would rather do, and a guy who shows up to take care of a woman he hardly knows, giving me something I've never before had in my life.

Yes, it's probably way too soon for me to like someone as much as I like Lucas, but there is no denying that I *do* like him and that I'm really looking forward to seeing him again.

Chapter 6

A New Dream

Lucas

"Are you sure you're good to keep an eye on her for a little while this afternoon?" I ask my brother's wife as Maddi heads straight for Muffin, Fawn's Irish wolfhound, who is sprawled out on the couch.

"I told you I was sure when you texted this morning. Levi told you I was sure when you called to ask him if I was really sure. I'm telling you once again—I'm sure. You know I love Maddi. It's not a hardship to spend time with her."

I run my hand across my jaw. I always feel guilty whenever I ask anyone in my family to watch Madeline for me. Since my divorce, they have all stepped in to help whenever I've needed it, but I hate feeling like I'm taking advantage of them.

"And you're going to Courtney's, right?" Fawn asks, a knowing smile playing on her lips.

"Yeah. She caught Maddi's bug, so . . ."

"So you're taking care of her because it's the nice thing to do." She rolls her eyes, and I laugh. "Maddi says she's pretty."

"She is pretty."

"I'm happy for you." She grins.

"I don't know that there is anything to be happy about yet," I admit.

She shakes her head, a knowing look in her eyes. "Even if nothing comes of this, I'm happy that you're willing to try again. You deserve to find a good woman, Lucas. I have no doubt that you *will* find someone worth your time. Someone who will love you and Maddi."

I haven't dated at all since my divorce. I haven't been willing to put myself out there, because I know that with me comes my daughter—that's more than a lot of women are looking for. I also refuse to have another woman come into her life who will only disappoint her.

"Thanks again for this. I'll be home in time for dinner."

"Don't rush." She winks, and I fight back a smile. I love Fawn. She is perfect for my brother, the hard to his soft and the crazy to his sane. She makes him happy—happier than I have ever seen him. It gives me hope that I might still find a woman to spend the rest of my life with.

"Come give me a kiss, honey. I'm gonna take off," I call across the room to Maddi.

She's sprawled out on top of Muffin, who is loving the attention. She skips across the room to me. Once she's close, I pick her up and wrap my arms around her in a hug.

"Love you. Be good."

"I'm always good." She grins, and I grin back. She *is* always good—except when she's being a hellion.

I kiss her cheek, then set her down. "Have fun."

Fawn smiles, and I give her a quick hug before taking off.

I stop off at the store and exchange the movies I rented yesterday at Redbox for new ones. I also pick up some bread and bananas and get myself a Danish and a coffee. When I make it to Courtney's twenty minutes later, I wonder if I should have called to tell her I was on my way. I push that thought aside and knock.

"Hey." She smiles at me through a small crack.

I frown, wondering if she checked her peephole before opening up. I wondered the same thing last night.

"Did you check to see it was me?" I ask as she steps back to let me inside.

"What?"

"You live alone in New York City. Did you check the peephole before you opened the door?"

"I . . ." She looks at the door, then me, clearly confused. "No one else but you and Abby has ever come by."

"You need to check who's here before you unlock your door, babe. It's not safe."

"Okay . . ."

The word is drawn out, and I can tell by the set of her brows that she's still confused. Hell, I'm confusing myself with my overprotective demand. When I was married to Eva—before we brought Maddi home—I didn't even worry about the door being locked when she was home alone.

"How are you feeling?" She looks better. Her color is back, and her eyes seem more alive than they did last evening.

"Better. A little tired, but a lot better."

"Good." I lean down and kiss her cheek, then move to the kitchen. "Have you eaten?" I ask over my shoulder.

"No. I got up just a few minutes ago. Sorry about passing out on you last night." She toys with the edge of her tank top like she's nervous.

"You needed to rest," I say, then hold up the bag of bread I brought with me. "How about some toast? It should be gentle enough on your stomach."

"Sure." She lifts her hands to her hair and frowns. "I'm going to do something with this mess so you don't have to look at it."

"You look gorgeous," I tell her. She does. Even when she's not feeling her best, she's still perfect.

"Thanks." She ducks her head in embarrassment. "I'll be right back."

I go about making her some tea and toast. When she comes back out of her bedroom, her beautiful hair is down. She's wearing a pair of tight black leggings—which show off everything—and a black tank top with a hoodie unzipped over it.

"Here you go." I hand her the tea and plate of toast after she settles on one of the chairs at the table just outside the kitchen. Taking a seat across from her, I sip my coffee and take out my apple Danish.

"Where's Maddi today?"

"With my brother's wife," I say.

She nods, looking thoughtful.

"Can I ask you something?" She sounds like she really doesn't want to ask whatever it is that's on her mind.

"Shoot." I relax back in the chair.

"Where is Maddi's mom?"

Fuck.

"You don't have to tell me. I was just curious, but it's none of my business." She looks away.

I study her, wondering how much I should tell her. Part of me doesn't want to taint what we are building by filling her in on my past, but if I want *her* to share with *me*, I know I'm going to have to do the same in return.

"Her mom lives with her boyfriend, in Connecticut. Since our divorce she's seen Maddi maybe a half dozen times. It sucks, because Maddi misses her—or rather misses the idea of her. She was never the most loving mom. Still, she's the only mom Maddi knows, so it hurts that she's not around."

"In a *year* she's only seen her daughter a half dozen times?" she asks, her voice filled with disbelief.

"Yeah."

"Why?"

"She's got a boyfriend who isn't hip on the idea of dating a woman with a kid. She doesn't have Maddi visit her, and she doesn't come to the city very often to see Maddi."

"Oh my god. You're not serious."

"I wish I wasn't." I take another sip of my coffee.

"I'm sorry."

"It's okay. I'm *not* sorry. I know I should be. I know that I should want her in our daughter's life, but when she was around, Maddi was always on edge, trying to be perfect because her mom expected her to be. She couldn't even laugh at the dinner table, because Eva considered that playing around and would get pissed. I didn't grow up like that, and I don't want my girl to grow up like that, either."

"I understand that, but it's still sad that she's going to grow up knowing that her mom didn't put her first."

"Yeah." I nod my agreement. "My mom's great, and my brothers' wives are awesome, though. They all try to make up for the loss."

"That's good. I'm glad you have that. That *she* has that." She looks over her shoulder when soft music starts up. "That's my cell. I left it by my bed. I'll be right back." She gets up, and when she comes back she has the phone to her ear. She stops a foot from me and the table.

"I'm really okay. No, I'll be in tomorrow . . ." A pause. "Yes, I'm sure . . ." Another pause. "Really, I'm fine. Lucas is here." Her eyes widen right after she says my name. "Uhh . . . the guy who did the plans for my house." She pauses. "I can't talk about that—he's here. Yes." Her cheeks darken, and her eyes skitter past my shoulder. "Abby, seriously. You are *not* coming over." Her head falls back to her shoulders. "Seriously. Do not show up. Oh god." She pulls the phone from her ear and drops her eyes to her feet.

"Everything okay?"

"I . . ." She lifts her head to look at me. "Right now, yes. But in about ten minutes probably not—because Abby is coming over to check you out."

"She's worried about you?"

"Yeah." She lifts one delicate shoulder. "She represented me during my divorce and knows what I went through with my ex, so she's a little protective."

"How long ago did you get divorced?"

"We finalized about eight months ago, but we had been separated for a few months before that."

"Why?"

"Why?" she repeats.

It's like she didn't hear my question, but I know she did. She's stalling.

"Yeah. Why'd you get divorced?"

Her jaw gets tight, so I expect her not to answer. But she does.

"He cheated and got another woman pregnant."

"Motherfucker."

"Yep." She nods in agreement. "So Abby knows all of that and is also a little bit of a man hater because of what she's seen in her job. She's sweet, but she'll probably be inappropriate and ask a million personal questions. She's assuming that since you're here, there is something going on between us."

"There *is* something going on between us," I state.

I watch as her whole body jerks and her eyes widen.

"What?"

"Don't get me wrong, I would have still checked on you last night when I found out you were sick if I wasn't interested . . . but I wouldn't have sat with you through a movie, watched you sleep through another, carried you to bed, and fought myself to keep from kissing you."

"I . . . You . . . I . . . We . . ." She finally snaps her mouth closed, and her eyes focus on my growing smile.

"Yep, that about sums it up," I agree.

She rolls her lips together; then they lift at the corners.

Sitting back, I watch her smile slowly slide away. Her eyes leave mine, and she speaks. "I don't know if I'm ready for anything serious, Lucas."

"I'm not asking you to marry me," I say. Her eyes meet mine once more. "I'm just asking to spend some time getting to know you. And to have you get to know me—and my daughter, if it comes to that. We don't have to rush into anything, but you can't stand there and tell me you aren't interested in me. Or not at least a little bit curious about where this could go."

"You're really straightforward."

"Not normally, but I can tell that's what you need from me."

"What does that mean?"

"I knew before you told me what a dick your ex was that you had been hurt. I can tell that you need me to be up-front with you about what I want, or what I'm asking of you."

I watch her swallow. "Why?"

"Why?"

"Yes. Why are you interested in me?"

"Because you're beautiful, sweet, and make me laugh. Because you stepped up to help me out without question. Because I like you. I like spending time with you, and I want to do that more."

"I come with a lot of baggage."

"Babe, my own bags are heavy as fuck. You aren't the only one with shit to carry," I tell her.

Her expression softens in understanding.

"I like you, too," she says.

I reach out and pull her closer, to stand between my thighs.

"That's a good place to start. So what do you say? Are you willing to get to know me?"

"Yes." Her eyes stay locked on mine.

"Good." My eyes drop to her mouth when she sways toward me.

I start to slide my hand around her hip to pull her even closer, but end up laughing when there's a simultaneous knock at the door.

Her head falls back in frustration.

I point out the obvious. "I think your friend's here."

She rolls her eyes at me before she lets me go and moves to the front door. She opens it without looking through the peephole. *Again.* "You know . . ."

She starts; then I watch her back straighten and her shoulders fill with tension. I can't see who's at the door, but I can tell by her reaction that it's not who she expected it to be. "Tom."

Tom? Is he her ex? The guy who cheated on her and got another woman pregnant while she was married to him?

"What are you doing here?"

"Mom told me you weren't feeling great. I wanted to come make sure you were okay," a man's voice answers.

I get up and move toward the door—and into view. My eyes scan the guy. He looks like money. He's almost as tall as me. Thin, wearing an expensive tailored suit, shiny shoes, and a glinting gold watch. He looks surprised when he sees me.

"Who is *he*?"

"You came all the way from Boston to check on me?" Courtney asks, ignoring Tom's question. "Seriously? You never even called home to check on me if I was sick when we were still living together."

"Who is *he*?" Tom repeats.

Courtney steps slightly to the side and looks at me over her shoulder. "He's—"

"Her boyfriend," I state, not giving a fuck that I just told her that we would take this slow.

No way is Tom going to just show up and think that he still has a shot with her.

"Boyfriend? You're *dating*?" Tom asks, looking wounded.

"This is not happening, Tom. Go home to your girlfriend—and your child." She starts to shut the door.

"I'm not with Stephanie anymore." He places his hand against the door. "I couldn't be with her when I'm still in love with you."

Her body gets tighter. Seeing her in distress, I move in closer and press myself against her back, rest my hand on her hip.

"I want another shot. I want to fix this. I want to fix *us*."

"No." She attempts to shut the door again, but he doesn't move his hand to let her.

"Is this because of *him*?" he asks, jerking his chin in my direction.

"No. It's because you are a lying, cheating dick. Now leave."

"What's going on here?" a petite brunette asks, pushing her way into the apartment between Tom and Courtney.

"It's none of your concern," Tom states. His eyes move back to Courtney. "I'm not leaving until we talk." His eyes slice to the woman who just showed up, then to me. "Alone."

"Sorry, buddy, but I'm not leaving you alone with my woman. Especially when it's obvious she doesn't want to be alone with you."

"*Your* woman?" His lip curls up in disgust.

"*My* woman." I shrug, then pull Courtney back a step. "Like she said—leave."

"This is . . . This is . . ." He looks at me, then his eyes move to my hand. It's still on Courtney's hip. They narrow.

"Over," I say, pulling Courtney back another step and then moving forward slightly into his space, forcing both women behind me. "If Courtney wants to talk to you, she has your number. Until she calls, you leave her be." I shut the door in his red face, then sigh when he starts to pound against it on the other side.

"That was awesome," says the woman who must be Abby. I turn around. "Seriously, you have my approval just for that."

"Abby . . ." Courtney shakes her head.

"Well, that whole 'she's my woman' thing was hot—and even hotter because it totally pissed off your dickhead ex-husband."

"I can't believe that he showed up here," Courtney whispers, looking at the door Tom has finally stopped pounding on.

"Did you tell his mom you were sick?" Abby questions before frowning.

"I mentioned yesterday that I was feeling a little off when we talked in the morning."

"Why?"

"Why?" Courtney's brows pull together over her beautiful eyes.

"Yeah. Why did you tell his mom that?"

"You know why. She's been like a mom to me. Never in a million years would I have thought that he would use that as an excuse to show up here."

"You're tight with his family?" I question.

"I was. I . . . It's been strained since we got divorced, but I love his mom. We were close, really close."

My heart hurts once more for her. I don't know what it was like for her growing up, but I'm wondering if she longs for connection. If she's looking for love and acceptance and everything else that comes along with having a family.

"You don't want to lose that," I say.

She nods, and her eyes start to tear up.

"Don't cry."

"I won't," she lies.

I wrap my hand gently around her cheek and sweep away a stray tear.

"Would you mind if I took off to track him down and kick his ass?" I half joke.

Her lips twitch into a sad smile.

"Would you get into trouble if you did that?"

"Maybe. Then again, my brother's a cop in the city. So maybe not."

"Well then . . ." She moves for the door like she's going to open it. I laugh, burying my face in the crook of her neck while wrapping my arms around her.

"Um, hello? I'm still here," Abby says.

Courtney's body gets tight against mine like she'd forgotten someone else was there besides us.

With a sigh, I pull my face from her neck; I keep my arm wrapped around her, though.

"Abby?" I stick out my hand toward her.

"Yes. You must be Lucas." She shakes my hand, and I'm surprised by how firm her grasp is. "So you're together." She looks between Courtney and me, raising a brow.

"Well . . . ," Courtney starts hesitantly.

"We're getting to know each other." I give Courtney's shoulder a squeeze.

"You said she's your woman." Abby calls me out on my earlier words while narrowing her eyes slightly on me.

"She is." I shrug. I see Courtney's head tip up to look at me, but I don't look down at her.

"So she's 'your woman,' but you're still just getting to know her?"

"Abby . . ." Courtney sighs.

"I'm just trying to figure out what's going on here," Abby says to Courtney before she looks at me once more. "You should know that if you hurt her, I will hurt you. And by 'hurt you,' I mean I will take away your manhood and make it impossible for you to ever father a child."

"He already *has* a daughter," Courtney says.

Abby's eyes fill with surprise.

"He's also raising her on his own, basically."

"Oh." She shifts her gaze back and forth between Courtney and me, and her smile is surprisingly sweet. "Well then . . . what do you have to eat? I'm starving. I rushed over here from yoga."

She turns for the kitchen, and I watch her go.

I look down at Courtney when I feel her body start to shake.

When I see she's laughing, I fight a smile of my own. "What's funny?"

"I think you just got her approval."

"Really?"

"Yeah."

"Hmm."

"Thank you." At her soft tone, I search her eyes.

"For what?"

"For helping to get rid of Tom."

"You really don't have to thank me for that."

I tip my head farther down toward her. Her eyes drop to my mouth. My stomach dips, and I tighten my grip on her waist as she starts to get up on her tiptoes.

Just then Abby asks loudly, "Do you have any more of these? They are awesome!"

With a sigh and a grumbled statement I can't quite make out, Courtney descends until she's flat on her feet again, then moves toward the kitchen. "That Danish you're eating is Lucas's."

"Oh." Abby gives me a sheepish smile as she chews and swallows the bite she just took. "Sorry."

"It's all good."

"He *might* just be one of the good ones," she tells Courtney. "He's not even mad that some woman he hardly knows threatened to take his manhood and is now eating his food."

"Don't you have to work today?" Courtney asks.

"Nope. Sundays are for Jesus and relaxation."

"You told me that you don't believe in organized religion."

"I don't, but I still believe in god. I still do my duty to him by taking Sundays off." She takes another bite of the Danish she's still holding.

"You're still eating Lucas's Danish," Courtney points out.

"It's really good," Abby says around a mouthful. "I haven't had carbs in forever." She looks at me and holds out what looks like a bite and a half. "Do you want the rest?"

"I learned at an early age not to get between a woman and her carbs. Enjoy it. It's yours." I walk past Courtney, letting my hand glide across her hip as I go to the kitchen.

"Do you think Tom is planning on sticking around the city?" Abby asks as she takes a seat at the table with Courtney.

I put a couple of slices of bread into the toaster.

"I have no idea. Hopefully not."

"We can file a—" Abby starts.

My eyes fly to Courtney when she cuts her off sharply. "I can't do that."

"Babe, you can." Abby grabs her hand. "I know you don't want to, but if he won't let you be . . ."

"Does he show up a lot?" I ask, surprised by the growl in my own voice.

"No . . . Well, not since I moved from Boston. I haven't seen him since then."

"He keeps calling you. You told me yourself that he's calling all the time," Abby says as I spread butter on my toast.

I don't like what I'm hearing one bit.

"I don't answer when he calls. It's not a big deal." Courtney sighs.

Abby lets out a frustrated huff. "Fine, but if he does anything *at all* that makes you feel uncomfortable, I want to know about it."

"It will be okay . . . ," Courtney tries again.

"You're only saying that because you haven't seen what I have. I know how men like him get when they don't get what they want."

Courtney gives in. "If anything happens, I will let you know. Then we will talk about what to do going forward."

I feel my body relax.

"That's good enough for now," Abby agrees, letting Courtney's hand go before she shoves the rest of my Danish in her mouth. "Now, what are you two up to today?" She looks at me.

"Courtney's going to rest," I state. Then I add, "I got a couple movies, so I figured we'd hang on the couch." I look at Courtney. "That okay with you?"

"That sounds good to me," she agrees with a small smile.

I carry my toast to the table and take a seat.

"I could join you," Abby says as she smiles evilly.

Courtney shakes her head. "No."

"No? You don't want me here, hanging out with you two while he 'gets to know you' as *his* woman?" She raises a brow.

"Not even a little bit," Courtney says.

I laugh.

"Fine. I guess I should be on my way. I have some errands I want to run before I head home." She stands and kisses Courtney on the cheek before looking at me. "It was nice to meet you, Lucas. I can honestly say that isn't a lie."

"Same."

When she's gone, I return my attention to Courtney.

"You okay?"

"Yeah."

"That scene with your ex was extreme."

"Yeah," she agrees again while pulling in a deep breath. I notice that she's not really looking at me.

"Wanna talk about it?"

"He said he left her," she says.

My stomach drops.

"What the hell is wrong with him? Why would he do that—not only to her, but to his *child*? I haven't . . ." She shakes her head before meeting my gaze. "I haven't ever told him that I would consider taking him back. Not once."

"Would you?"

"Would I?" She frowns.

"Yeah. Would you take him back?"

"No. I mean, when I first found out about his affair I was scared to death. The life we had planned was ending, so I wondered what I did wrong. For about ten minutes I convinced myself that I could fix us . . . before I realized there was nothing to fix. He destroyed what we had."

"Did you know about the baby then?"

"I didn't find out until a month after I learned about the affair. *He* didn't tell me about it, either. His mistress did when I ran into her at the grocery store, of all places. She was all too happy to share her good news with me. I don't know if getting pregnant was part of her plan, but . . ." Her words taper off. "In the end, it didn't matter. That was just the icing on the cake."

"I'm sorry you had to deal with that." I reach for her hand and rub my thumb over the soft skin on her wrist.

"I . . . I know I should be sorry, too, but I'm not. I was trying to hold on to him when I should have been letting go. What happened forced me to let go. Don't get me wrong—it hurt. I built a life with him, made plans with him. I wanted the dream he promised me, but in the end it was harder losing the dream than it was losing him," she says, her eyes locked on our intertwined hands.

"I understand that."

"You do?" She looks up at me.

"I do. I had always wanted a family, so when I found out Maddi's mom was pregnant I latched on to the idea of building a life with her. I knew she wasn't the kind of woman to give me a solid foundation, but I still tried because I wanted that dream. It sucked when things came to an end, but I was also glad I no longer had to live a lie."

"We sound kind of depressing," she jokes with a smile, causing me to smile in return.

"What do you say we stop talking about our exes and watch a movie?"

"I'd say that sounds like a plan," she agrees.

We both get up. She clears our dishes while I set up the movie—a comedy that I hope will lighten the mood.

When she takes a seat on the couch, I take a seat next to her and wrap my arm around her shoulders, curling her into my side.

"This movie sucks," I tell her forty minutes later. Her body starts to shake, and then she presses her face into the side of my chest. She's snorting with laughter.

"It's a movie about hot dogs!" she snorts again. "What did you expect?"

"I guess I had my hopes up."

I press "Stop" on the remote.

"You had your hopes up about an adult cartoon that features talking meat products and produce?" She giggles, and I chuckle.

"Basically." I lift my hand to her cheek.

All the humor leaves her face as her eyes search mine.

"Lucas?"

"Yeah?" I drop my eyes to her lips just as her pink tongue darts out to swipe the bottom one.

"Will you kiss me?"

I growl as I lean in and capture her mouth. Her lips part, and my tongue slips in. The first taste of her has my cock jumping against the zipper of my jeans. She tastes like peppermint and her own unique flavor—something I know I could come to crave. Hearing her moan and feeling her fingers dig into my shoulder cause me to lose it. I lay her back onto the couch and cover her with my body. I deepen the kiss while her legs wrap around my hips and her hands slide up my back.

Fuck, she can kiss.

She feels good under me—all soft and all woman. I grind myself against her, then pull back and look down at her. She's beautiful when she's turned on. Her cheeks are flushed, her eyes dark with want, her breathing erratic.

God, I want her.

Before I screw this up by going too fast, I sit back and pull her up with me.

"You stopped," she complains breathily.

I smile.

Fuck, she's cute. And so damn sweet.

"I know, but I told you we'd go slow. I meant that when I said it."

"Oh . . . right." She bites her lip, and I groan while adjusting myself.

"As much as I don't want to go, I think I should," I tell her as I wrap my hand around the side of her neck and rest my forehead against hers. "How about dinner on Tuesday?"

"You're *leaving*?" There is no missing the disappointment in her expression or voice.

"I don't trust myself to stick around and keep my promise at the same time. So yeah, baby. I'm gonna go," I say.

Her eyes widen as they drop to my lap—and my obvious erection.

"Exactly. So what do you say? Does dinner Tuesday work for you?"

"That works for me."

I touch my mouth to hers in a soft kiss before pulling away and forcing myself to put distance between us. I head for the door.

"I'll see you Tuesday, but I'll call tonight when Maddi goes to bed."

"Sure. Um . . . Thank you again for today. It was nice."

"Yeah. Nice." I move my eyes over her, then open the door. I have to bite back a groan. She's just too damn pretty. "Don't forget to lock up after me, and check your peephole if anyone knocks."

"Right." She bites her lip.

I can't fight it. I start back across the room, and she rushes at me. My mouth opens over hers, and I thrust my tongue between her lips, kissing her hard.

"Tuesday," I say when I jerk my mouth from hers.

"Tuesday," she pants.

I push her away and leave without another look—because I know I won't be able to go if I see the warm look in her eyes again.

As I head down in the elevator, I wonder if she might just be the kind of woman who'd give me the foundation I need to build a new dream.

Chapter 7

Date Number Eight, and Falling in Love

Courtney

"What are your plans tonight? Do you want to get a drink after work?" Abby asks as we catch a cab back to the office from the home of a potential new client. The woman is looking to divorce her husband and leave him for another man. Since she entered the marriage with more money than her husband, though, she doesn't want to lose it all. I really do not understand the way people think. I can't understand why some people cheat. Why not just end your relationship before looking elsewhere? "Earth to Courtney . . ." Abby nudges my shoulder with hers.

"Sorry. What was that?" I look up at her, then hear my phone ping with an incoming message.

"Drinks tonight?"

"I can't. I'm having dinner with Lucas," I say while texting him back about where we're meeting.

It's Tuesday, and two days since he left my apartment after kissing me so passionately that I couldn't think straight for the rest of the evening. Never in my life had I been kissed like that. He made me forget *everything* when he kissed me. I bet if you had asked me my name just afterward, I wouldn't have been able to tell you.

"Where are you guys going?"

I look up from my phone after I press "Send."

"A small Italian place between his apartment and mine."

"Convenient if you don't want the night to end." She wiggles her brows, and I roll my eyes.

"We're just having dinner. He has full custody of his daughter, so he has to get home to her. There won't be any of *that*."

At least not yet, anyway, I leave out.

"Is she going to be at dinner?" Abby asks.

"No. He asked his brother to look after her for a couple hours while we are out."

Even though I've already met Maddi, I'm starting to get the idea that I won't see her again unless things between Lucas and me progress. Really, I respect him so much more for thinking about her feelings.

"What was she like?" she asks.

"She's beautiful and sweet. A total daddy's girl." I smile.

"I like this for you."

I let out a breath. I like it, too. I'm also scared out of my mind.

"You're worried?" She reads my expression.

"Terrified. You know what happened to me. I . . . This is all so sudden. I just don't know if I'm ready."

"You like him."

"I do. He gets me. And he's sweet and understanding." I sigh dreamily.

"And hot." Her eyes light up.

"Yes . . . hot. God, so hot." I let my head fall back against the leather headrest. "I don't even know why he's interested in me."

"Um, because you're beautiful and sexy and sweet and generous and loving and—"

"Okay, you can stop." I shake my head while a smile twitches my lips.

"Not until you tell me that you understand why he's interested in you."

"I understand," I lie.

I didn't used to be so jaded, but having a man cheat who's supposed to love you makes you question your own self-worth.

Abby presses her lips together in disapproval, then waves her hand at me. "You know what? I'm not even going to get into this with you. I have a feeling that Lucas is the kind of man who will make it perfectly clear why he's into you."

"What does that mean?"

"Just mention to him that you are unworthy of his greatness, and you'll see." She shrugs; then her eyes fill with mischief. "Also record his reaction on your cell phone so I can see."

"Are one of you gonna pay?" the cab driver asks, impatiently breaking into our conversation. I see that we are parked in front of our office building.

"Sorry," I mumble, reaching for my wallet.

Abby gets out her card before I can get mine and swipes it through the machine. We both get out and head into the building. Before I know it, it's time to leave for the evening.

∾

"I really love this dress." Lucas groans against my skin while pressing me harder against the wall next to my apartment door. I smile as he slides his hands down my hips and over my dress.

"You said that already."

He stops kissing my neck and looks down at me.

"It's a really fucking great dress." He grins, and I bite my bottom lip.

His eyes told me that he liked my dress the moment we met outside the restaurant. Then he told me again with his mouth when I was sitting across from him. Then he told me *again* as he walked me down the block to my building while holding my hand.

Dinner was good, but his company was better. I have never met anyone else in my life who I can talk to about nothing and everything. I also have never met another man who's made me feel as beautiful and as wanted as he does with a single look or touch.

"I wish I didn't have to get home," he says as his eyes roam over my face.

I drop my forehead to his shoulder and let out a deep breath.

"Me too."

I give his waist a squeeze, hating that he has to leave but knowing it's for the best. It would be so easy to give myself over to him without thinking about what I was doing, but I know I'm not ready for that. Not yet.

"Thank you for dinner." I look up at him.

"My pleasure." His lips touch mine, and I fight the urge to open my mouth and deepen the kiss. "I'm taking you out again Friday, so don't make plans."

"What about Maddi?" I ask.

He smiles. "She's sleeping over at her friend's place—the one who had the party last weekend."

My face softens. "Is she excited?"

"She got the invite Monday and hasn't stopped talking about it. So yeah, she's excited."

"Good." I lean up and press my lips to his, unable to stop myself.

"Damn, I really wish I didn't have to leave." His forehead rests against mine briefly before he lets me go with one last, soft kiss. "I'll see you Friday."

"You will." I smile at that, then open my door and back into my apartment while keeping my eyes locked with his. "Have a good night, Lucas."

"You too, baby."

I watch him walk away, then close the door and get up on my tip-toes to look at him through the peephole—like a total creeper. When he gets in the elevator, his eyes lock on my door. I swear he knows that I'm watching him. Only when the elevator doors close and he's out of sight do I head for my bedroom to get out of my dress and heels.

I settle in bed against the headboard and grab my cell phone. I smile when I see a good-night text from Lucas. I text him back.

Then I feel my chest get tight when I notice that Tom's mom called and left me a voice mail. I haven't spoken to her since the day Tom showed up here. I don't know why I haven't, I just . . . I guess I feel like I need to put some distance between us. It's something I've been thinking about for a while now. I love her, and it sucks that I need to let her go, but it has to happen if I'm ever going to be completely rid of Tom. I don't want him in my life. If I have to let her go to get that, then that's what I'm going to have to do. Holding my phone, I debate with myself whether I should just delete the voice mail. Instead, I click on the "Play" icon and put my cell on speaker.

"Hey, honey. It's Mom . . ."

Mom. God, I loved it when she referred to herself that way toward me. She *has* been like a mom for the last few years. She's been stable, loving, accepting, and understanding. Tears fill my eyes.

"I . . . Well, Tom got back yesterday. He told me that he came to see you and that you had a man at your place." She inhales an audible breath. "I guess until he told me that, I hadn't . . . Well, I guess I had been secretly holding out hope that you two would find a way to work things out and get back together." She pauses for so long that I start to wonder if she hung up. "I get it. More than you know. I get it, and I don't blame you for making the choices that you've made." Her voice drops to a whisper. "I wish I was as strong as you. I love you. Don't forget that."

I swear I hear tears in her voice before the message comes to an end and a digital voice asks if I want to delete it.

I close my eyes, which *are* filled with tears, and my heart hurts for her. I remember Tom mentioning years ago his dad's cheating on her. At the time, I didn't think anything of it because they seemed to be okay. Now I wonder how many times it happened. How many times she let her husband's infidelities go and looked the other way. No doubt she died a little inside each time she did it. She told me I should forgive Tom for what he did to me, and maybe she said that because that's what she did.

I swipe away the wetness on my cheeks and let my finger hover over her number. Part of me wants to call her, but part of me knows I shouldn't. Just when I think I couldn't dislike Tom more than I already do, I'm proven wrong. Because of him I have to reevaluate my relationship with the only woman who has ever been a mother to me.

I decide to text her.

Lorie, I got your voice mail. I love you, too. I'll call to check in soon.

I press "Send" before I can talk myself out of doing it. Then I drop my cell to the bedside table, turn out the lamp, and lie down. I hear my cell phone buzz, and I pick it up, expecting to see a reply from Lorie.

It's a message from Lucas.

Still thinking about that dress, you in that dress, you in that dress wearing those heels. Really I can't stop thinking about you.

That wasn't even my best dress. Wait until you see what I have planned for Friday ;)

I'm looking forward to that, baby. Sweet dreams.

Back at you.

71

I drop my phone to my bedside table. Even with Lorie's words still ringing through my head, I fall asleep with a smile on my face.

~

"What the hell is wrong?" Abby asks.

I look up from my phone and know without a doubt my eyes are filled with fear.

"Lucas wants me to have dinner with him and Madeline tonight." I let her read the text I just got from Lucas. A text where he *told* me, rather than *invited* me, to have dinner with him and Madeline at a pizza place near his apartment.

Her eyes scan the message, then move to my face. "And?" She shrugs.

"And . . ." I shake my head. "I can't have dinner with them. It's too soon!" I cry in distress. It *is* too soon, or in my head it's too soon. Me having dinner with Maddi and Lucas is a huge step. A giant one. Yes, I have always wanted kids, but I never thought I would be dating a man with a child. I don't know how to navigate this kind of thing.

"You've met her before, babe. It's not a big deal." Abby's words pull me from my mental freak-out.

"Yeah, but that was before I had her dad's tongue down my throat and his hand up my . . ." My eyes widen.

"His hand where?" Abby smirks, and my face gets hot . . . or hotter. "How many dates is this now?"

"If you count him coming over to take care of me when I was sick, eight." Last Friday we had dinner again, and when it was over he took me home. We made out on my couch until almost three in the morning, then he left. The next day, Saturday—less than five hours later—he brought me a coffee and a bagel. We hung out and went to a movie before he had to pick up Madeline from her friend's house. I didn't see him Sunday because he spent the day with Madeline, but I did see him Monday. We had lunch together in the afternoon, after meeting the contractors at my house. I saw him again on Thursday evening for dinner.

"Eight. So it's not just date number four, it's date number *eight*. He probably knows by now that you have staying power. He wants to see you with his daughter to make sure he's right."

"So you're telling me this is basically a test? That if things don't go well, I won't be seeing Lucas again?" My stomach hurts at the idea. "That doesn't make me feel any better, Abby."

"The fact that you're worried about this means that you care about him. It will be fine. Don't stress about it."

"That's easy for you to say. You're not the one who's falling for a guy—and could ruin it all without even realizing it," I grumble. She laughs. "I should take her something to win her over. What do six-year-old girls like?"

"Girl stuff," she says unhelpfully. I frown.

"I'll check online and see what I can find." I turn toward my computer, drag the mouse to the search bar, and google my question.

"What are those?" Abby asks, leaning over next to me after I click on one of the long lists of suggestions.

"I have no idea. They kind of look like dolls." They do look like dolls, but with pudgy bodies and huge eyes. They come inside a ball that you have to break open before you know which one you get.

"Kids nowadays are so weird."

"Yeah, says the woman who probably wore a pacifier necklace when she was a kid because everyone else did."

"Touché." She smiles down at me. "I did love those, though. And slap bracelets, Pogs, and troll dolls."

"They seem like they are pretty popular. Maybe I will get her a few of them." I click on a website where they are for sale.

"Holy cow. Ten dollars for a three-inch plastic ball and baby? Are they crazy?"

"Don't think of the money; think about me winning her six-year-old heart over."

"Bribery. I like it." She grins, and I look up at her, then smile back before looking at the clock.

"If I'm going to get to the toy store, I'm going to have to leave in about ten minutes. Are you okay? Do you need me to stick around?"

"There is nothing else on the agenda for the day. Do you want me to come with you?"

"Yes," I answer immediately. "Then you can help me figure out what to wear."

"What's wrong with what you have on?" Her eyes move over my dress—a dress similar to the one I wore on my first dinner date with Lucas.

It's not revealing, but I don't think that matters to him. He likes it when I wear dresses, and I don't want to be sitting across from him and his daughter wondering what dirty things he's thinking about me in my dress. After our date last Friday, when we were back at my apartment, he described in vivid detail everything he wanted to do to me in that dress while he brought me to orgasm with his mouth against mine—and his hand between my legs, and up that dress.

"Nothing, I just need to look more . . ." I stop to search for the right word.

"Motherly?" she suggests.

I bite my lip while shrugging.

"Fine. After we go find these ridiculous and expensive toys, we will go to your place and find you something to wear."

"Perfect," I agree. "Go get your bag."

An hour later we have three dolls. Forty minutes after that, we are back at my place so I can change to go meet Lucas and Madeline.

~

Wearing a pair of dark boot-cut jeans, a fitted scoop-neck rose-colored T-shirt, and my brown suede wedge sandals, I get out of the cab. I head toward the entrance of Princess Pizza, where Lucas asked me to meet him. The shop is adorable—the walls are two different shades of pink, with drawings that kids obviously did framed and hanging on the walls.

"Can I help you?" a gorgeous brunette asks from behind the counter as soon as her eyes lock with mine.

"I'm meet—" I start, but am quickly cut off.

"Hey, baby." I hear Lucas's deep voice, and then I feel his arm wrap around my waist and his lips touch my cheek. I turn and focus on his handsome face. I smile, feeling the anxiety and nervousness that have been plaguing me since he told me our plans for the evening wash clean away.

"Courtney?" The woman behind the counter says my name, and I look at her, blinking in surprise that she knows who I am. "Maddi is right. You're really pretty." She smiles.

"I—"

"Baby, this is my sister-in-law's sister Libby. Libby, this is Courtney," Lucas introduces us.

"Nice to meet you." I give her a smile, and she gives me a broad grin while her curious eyes shoot back and forth between us.

"You too," she murmurs. A man steps up behind her, wrapping his hand possessively around her hip to hold her, much the same way Lucas is holding me. "This is my guy, Antonio." She tips her head back toward him. "Honey, this is Courtney. The lady Maddi's been talking about."

"Nice to meet you," Antonio says.

My lips part in astonishment. He's gorgeous—seriously gorgeous—and he and Libby make the perfect couple. Lord help them if they ever have a daughter, because they are going to have to invest in some serious manpower to keep the boys away from her.

"Where is Madeline?" I ask Lucas, looking around for her.

"She's in the back, helping with the pizza dough for a party tomorrow," Libby answers. "I'll send her out to you guys. Lucas already placed an order for a pepperoni pizza, but just let me know if you want something else."

"Pepperoni is perfect," I assure her.

"I got you a Diet Coke at the table," Lucas tells me before he takes my hand and leads me to a booth in the back of the restaurant.

"This place is really cute," I tell him as I take a seat in the booth. He sits across from me.

"Yeah, Libby did a good job when she took over the place. She's quietly building a name for herself, and the place hasn't even been open six months."

"She mentioned a pizza party?"

"She has a back room that people can rent out, and kids can make their own pizzas."

"That's really cool."

"It is. Maddi is anxious for her party, too. Libby's hosting it here in a few weeks. She already sent out the invites," he says, and then his eyes roam over me, making me shift in my seat. "You look beautiful."

"Thanks."

"Even in jeans," he says as his voice drops to a deep growl that I feel all over. "You're the sexiest woman I have ever seen."

"Lucas."

"Your ass is amazing in jeans."

"Seriously?" I know my cheeks are red.

"Babe, you can't expect me not to notice."

"Okay. Well, can you notice but not say anything?"

"I can try." He gives me a devilish smile—one that says he actually *won't* try, not even a little.

"You're here."

I look over my shoulder and watch Madeline skip-hop toward our table from across the room. She's in sneakers, jeans, and a T-shirt that is the same blue as her eyes. Her long hair is pulled up in a ponytail, and she has a large smile on her face.

"Hey, sweetheart." I slide to the edge of the booth, wanting to hug her but not sure it's the right thing to do. "It's so good to see you feeling better." I reach out and take hold of her hand.

"It's good to be feeling better." She grins at me. "Did Daddy tell you that I got to make our pizza?"

"He didn't." I look at Lucas and see that his eyes are soft as he looks at his daughter.

"I did." She smiles, then adds, "I also made it with extra cheese."

"Now I *know* it's going to be the best pizza I have ever had in my life. I love cheese."

"Me too." She grins, then plops down right next to me—*me* instead of her dad, making my heart turn over in my chest.

"I . . . Well, I brought you something," I say, unsure all of a sudden. I wonder if I'm stepping over some kind of unwritten boundary.

"You did?" she asks while Lucas asks the same thing from across the table.

I ignore him and keep my eyes on Madeline.

"Yeah." I open my purse and pull out three round balls: one yellow, one baby blue, and one pale pink. "I read that these were the 'in' thing."

"Oh my god," she breathes, looking at the balls I set in front of her. "L.O.L. Surprise Dolls." Her eyes come to me and, before I can prepare myself, she throws her small body against mine. "Thank you."

I hug her back and silently vow then and there to buy her a million of them—even a few of the giant ones that cost fifty dollars apiece.

"You're welcome, sweetheart," I say. I meet Lucas's thoughtful gaze from across the table and give him a small smile.

"This is so cool," Madeline says, taking one of the balls from her dad, who stopped them from rolling off the table when she hugged me.

"You'll have to explain to me exactly what they are. I hadn't ever heard of them until today," I tell her.

She grins at me. "I'll show you." She breaks the seal on the pink one, exposing compartments with tiny bags shoved inside before popping the ball open. Pulling out a small plastic doll with big eyes, she dresses it with the stuff in the bags. Watching her smile and laugh, I can't help but to do the same. "Cool, right?" She holds up the now-dressed doll for me to see.

"Very cool. So do you ever get doubles?" I ask, looking at the other two balls she has yet to open.

"Sometimes, but me and my friends trade if we do."

"When I was a kid we had Pogs, these paper disks that came in a package. We'd trade with friends if we had the same ones, too."

"Pogs?" Lucas says, and I look up to see him grinning at me. "Showing your age, baby."

"Whatever." I roll my eyes at him, listening to him laugh.

"Daddy, can I go show Libby what Courtney got me?" Madeline asks as soon as she's unwrapped the other two toys.

"Sure, honey." He nods.

She gets up, smiling at me one more time before skipping toward the front counter, where Libby is standing and talking with an older woman with red hair.

"Trying to buy my girl?" At Lucas's question, my head flies around and my heart drops to my stomach.

"I . . ."

"I get why you did it, but you don't have to." He reaches across the table to hold my hand. "She likes you already."

"She does?"

"She said she likes your voice—and how nice you were to her even after she puked on you."

"Oh."

"Relax, baby. I wouldn't have you here with us if I didn't know that you already belonged."

"That's what Abby said, too," I admit, dropping my eyes from his to toy with the napkin on the table.

"What else did Abby say?" he asks.

I look up. "That this is a test . . ."

"Pardon?" He frowns.

"I mean . . . I mean, she thinks that you want to see me and Madeline together to see if this will work or not."

"Hmm." He looks over my shoulder.

I wonder what that *hmm* means, but I don't get a chance to ask, because Madeline shows back up, sliding in next to me right before a pink cake stand is placed in the middle of our table and our pizza is placed on top of it.

"Enjoy," says an older Hispanic gentleman with a wink before heading back to the front counter.

"Don't eat too much, honey. Remember we're going to get ice cream after we leave here," Lucas says as he slides a piece of pizza onto Madeline's plate.

"I'll leave room," she agrees, taking a bite as Lucas hands me my own slice.

I fold it in half—which is what you have to do with any good New York pizza—and take a bite, fighting back a groan of approval. It's delicious. The crust and the pepperoni are crisp, the sauce is sweet with a hint of spice, and the cheese is melted to perfection.

"This is the best pizza I have ever had," I tell Madeline. "The extra cheese is perfect."

Smiling at me proudly, she leans slightly into my side. In that moment, I fall a little bit in love with a little girl I hardly know.

∽

"I think she's out," I whisper to Lucas.

His eyes drop to his side, where Madeline is resting her head under his arm and against his chest.

"Pizza, ice cream, and a carriage ride did her in," he replies just as quietly.

I smile at him, then look down at his girl once more. "I think I'm in love with her."

"That's good, since the feeling is mutual."

I look up at him. Our eyes lock, and I see something in his gaze that makes me feel warm all over, like the sun when winter finally comes to an end or like lying under a blanket snuggled on the couch when it's snowing. It's comforting.

"Tonight has been amazing. Thank you for inviting me."

It *has* been amazing. First delicious pizza followed by awesome ice cream, then a carriage ride through the city—something I have wanted to do since I moved here but haven't been able to do because I didn't want to go alone. I never once felt like the third wheel with Madeline and Lucas. If anything, Madeline made me feel like I belonged with her and her dad. She always included me when she was talking, leaning into me and asking, "What do you think, Courtney?" or "Isn't that cool, Courtney?" Yes, it's safe to say I'm falling in love with her—and maybe even her dad.

When the carriage ride comes to an end, I climb down. Lucas gets out, holding a still-sleeping Madeline against his chest. My own chest warms and my throat gets tight as I watch him kiss the hair on top of her head, then look at me and smile.

Yes, I'm definitely feeling something for him.

"You should catch a cab and get her home," I tell him as we start walking down one of the few quiet backstreets in the city.

"Let's ride together. I'll have the driver drop you first," he says.

I nod, happy to have a few more minutes with him.

When we finally get a cab and settle into the back, he gives the driver directions to my place. He lets go of Madeline with one hand and links our fingers together. As I study his large hand holding mine, I fight back a sudden rush of emotion as another realization hits me. I've always craved affection. A soft touch as a reminder that I belong, that I'm wanted. Tom was somewhat—at the right time, in the right place—affectionate when we first got together, but as time went on he stopped touching me just to touch me and only really did it when it was time to have sex. It made me feel like I was being needy when I attempted to be affectionate with him for no other reason than to show I cared. With Lucas I'm finding that I never have to reach for him—because he's always there.

"You okay?" As I hear the concern in Lucas's voice, my eyes meet his.

"Yeah." I clear my throat. "Great, actually."

His eyes roam my face, and his expression fills with understanding. "What are your plans for tomorrow evening?"

"I'm thinking about going to the pound tomorrow. If I do find a dog, I might be attempting to win him or her over with lots of attention."

"You're gonna do that *tomorrow*?"

"Maybe." I shrug.

"Do you want me and Madeline to go with you?"

My eyes move to Madeline's sleeping face, and I slide some of her hair off her forehead, tucking it behind her ear.

"I'd like that, if you're not busy."

"We're just hanging around the house tomorrow. I know without even asking her that Madeline would love to go. Fawn has a dog that Madeline adores. She's always asking when she can get a puppy of her own, so this will be the next best thing."

"Then I'd love it."

"After we do that, we can go back to my place. I'll cook you dinner and wow you with my Hamburger Helper."

"A meal from a box has never sounded more appealing." I grin at him, and he smiles back just as the cab driver pulls up in front of my building.

"Kiss me, babe," he orders, holding my hand tighter as my other hand reaches for the door handle. My pulse skyrockets as I lean over the top of Madeline's head and place my mouth against his softly before pulling away. "Message when you're locked in. I'll call you as soon as I get her to bed."

"Sure," I agree.

He lets me go. I get out and head toward the front door, then look over my shoulder and see that the cab hasn't pulled away. Lucas's eyes are locked on me. With a small wave, I head inside and then go upstairs to my place.

I send Lucas a text, then get ready for bed. I'm looking forward to my phone call from him tonight—and seeing him and Maddi again tomorrow. I know I should be worried that we are moving too fast, that this is too good to be true, but I'm willing to take the risk. I'm willing to put myself out there because I know I will regret it if I don't at least see where this thing between Lucas and me will go.

Chapter 8

Unexpected Sleepover

Lucas

"What do you think of the name Merida?" Madeline asks.

I smile while I'm browning beef for my version of Hamburger Helper. I call it "my" version because I use the box's seasonings but add a can of cream of broccoli soup and a bag of mixed broccoli, cauliflower, and carrots. The first time I made it like this was in the hopes I could get Maddi to actually eat vegetables without throwing a fit. Thankfully, it worked.

"Like the princess from *Brave* with red hair?" Courtney asks.

I'm a little surprised that she knows the princess from a Disney movie—but also for some odd reason not surprised at all.

"Yes, she's my favorite. I want to learn to shoot a bow and arrow just like her," Madeline replies.

Both girls are lounging on the couch with the dog Courtney adopted today between them. The dog is round and short, with rusty-red hair that's curly in some spots and straight in others. With dark, wide-set eyes that are a little uneven and an underbite that shows off one missing tooth, the dog is so ugly she's kind of cute.

This morning, when I told Madeline what our plans were for the day, she was champing at the bit to get to Courtney's apartment. We ended up leaving our place an hour before we were supposed to. I made sure to call Courtney to let her know we were on our way, and when we got to her place she made us breakfast: pancakes, scrambled eggs, and bacon. The pancakes were in the shape of hearts. I knew Courtney made them that way just for Maddi, who loved them.

After eating and cleaning up, we went across town to the ASPCA. As soon as we arrived, we were taken to the kennels. I honestly didn't think Courtney would find a dog to adopt on the spot. I thought she would need some time to decide if she really wanted to own a dog, but I was wrong. As soon as the volunteer stopped in front of a scraggly-looking mutt and told us that the pup had been there for over five months without finding a home, *both* my girls fell in love. I suggested that we take the dog for a walk to make sure she was the right fit, so we took her to a park near the animal shelter. Courtney and Madeline played with her for over two hours. Watching both girls with smiles on their faces, running with the dog, throwing the ball, and just having fun, I knew that even if Courtney didn't adopt the dog, I would go back and pick her up. When we finally took her back inside, I wasn't surprised by Courtney's immediate decision to adopt. After we filled out the necessary paperwork, we went to the pet store for supplies before heading to my place. The moment we got in, both girls and the dog went to the couch. I started dinner.

"I think it's the perfect name. What do you think? Do you like the name Merida?" I look up and see that Courtney is addressing the dog, holding her furry red face in her hands. The dog licks at Courtney's face, causing her to laugh. "I think she likes it."

"Merida!" Maddi claps her hands to the tops of her thighs, and the dog rushes to her lap, licking her face and making her giggle.

"Do you want to watch *Brave*?" Madeline asks.

Courtney looks at my baby with a smile that is so sweet my chest actually aches just from the sight of it.

"Yes. I haven't seen it since it came out in theaters."

"YAY!" Maddi shouts. She shoots her hands up in the air while the newly named Merida woofs. She carefully scoots Merida off her lap and heads for her collection of movies.

As the movie starts up, I add the soup to the meat. I feel eyes on me, so I look over the peninsula in the kitchen. My breath catches when my eyes lock with Courtney's soft ones.

God, she's beautiful, and so damn sweet that she makes my jaw hurt like I've got a toothache.

If I didn't know it was too soon, I would swear that I was falling in love with her.

"Daddy, can I help make the crescent rolls when it's time?"

"Yeah, honey," I answer. Then I look at Courtney once more. "Babe, do you want some wine?"

"Yeah, but I'll get it."

"I got it." I go to the fridge and grab the bottle of wine I picked up for her. It's the same kind she had last Friday when we were out to dinner—a wine that I tasted on her lips as I brought her to orgasm on her couch.

I open the bottle and pour her a glass while wondering if it would be too much to ask Levi and Fawn to keep Maddi for me one night so that I can be alone with Courtney. A whole night of just us—in her bed or mine. Since my divorce I haven't even had the desire to have a woman sleep over or to spend the night out, but with Courtney I want that. I've enjoyed every moment I've spent with her. I love the way she can make me laugh without even trying. I love that she's easy to talk to and as laid back as I am. I can't get enough of her. Yes, I want her to get to know my daughter, but I also want to get to know Courtney—in every single way there is to know her. In *and* out of bed.

I take Courtney the glass of wine, letting my fingers linger on hers before I let go of it. Then I touch the top of Madeline's head and watch her smile up at me before I head back to the kitchen to finish up dinner for both my girls.

~

"Can Courtney read me a story tonight?"

At Madeline's question, my heart starts to beat oddly inside my chest. Since she was a baby, I have always been the one to read to her at night before tucking her in to sleep. She never even asked her mom to read to her. It's our thing.

"I . . ."

"Please, Daddy?"

Looking into her hope-filled eyes, I nod. "I'll see if she's up to it," I answer gruffly as she gets into bed and pulls the blankets up over her lap. "Courtney?" I call.

Two seconds later, she appears in the doorway. Her bare feet are sticking out from under her light jeans, which are molded to her from ankle to hip. She has a simple red T-shirt on. Her hair, which she wore down today, is now up in a messy bun on top of her head. When I see her so comfortable here and with Madeline, my heart stops its awkward thump and settles into a soft tempo.

"What's up?"

I realize I've been staring at her. "Madeline was asking if you'd like to read her a story tonight." At my question, her eyes flare and then fly to Madeline.

"I . . . ," she begins, unsure.

I hear the sound of nails clattering on the wood floor.

"Please?" Maddi begs, cutting in.

"Of course, sweetheart." She looks at me. "If you don't mind."

"I don't," I say, meaning it.

Merida slowly comes into the room and hops up onto the bed with Maddi, lying at her side and with her head on Maddi's stomach.

I stand up, and Courtney takes my place on the bed. My baby tugs her to lie down next to her, then cuddles up against her like she does me. Studying the two of them, I wonder if this is too much too soon. If I shouldn't pull back a little for Maddi's sake. But I can't seem to stop it. Really, I don't *want* to stop it.

"What are we reading?" Courtney asks.

Maddi picks up the book that she brought into bed with her.

"*The Princess and the Pea.* I love this book." Courtney smiles before she starts to read. I lean against the doorjamb, crossing my arms over my chest and my feet at the ankles. I watch both girls and the dog read the book together. The girls are both smiling, and the dog is in a happy trance because the top of her head is being rubbed. I pull myself away and go into the kitchen to grab a beer, then settle on the couch. I expect Courtney to come out of the room soon, so I turn on the news and start to watch.

I must doze off, because when I wake up one of the late-night talk shows is on. When I see the clock and the time, my gut gets tight. I wonder if Courtney saw me asleep and left without saying anything, not wanting to disturb me. I scan the apartment and see her purse on one of the barstools and her shoes near the door. I get up off the couch and go to Maddi's room. I stop in the doorway and lift my hand to my hair. Courtney and Maddi are snuggled together on Maddi's twin bed, asleep. Merida is passed out between them.

I turn off Maddi's bedside lamp and then scoop up a sleeping Courtney. She must be tired because she doesn't even twitch as I carry her out of the room. I move her to my bed and tuck her in. Going back to Maddi's room, I peek in and see that neither she nor Merida has moved. I leave them, turn off the TV and the lights, then go back to my bed. I get in with Courtney, pulling her against me. She mumbles something I can't make out before she burrows closer to my body before relaxing. Lying in the dark with her in my arms, I breathe in the smell of her shampoo and soak in her warmth. Eventually I fall asleep.

"Oh my."

I hear these whispered words, and my arms tighten instinctively as Courtney's soft warm body, tucked against mine, attempts to get away.

"Lucas."

"Go to sleep," I grumble, not ready to wake up and feeling more content than I have in years. Without even opening my eyes, I know it's way too early to get up.

"I . . . Are you awake?" she whispers.

"I don't want to be," I answer.

Her body gets stiff. "Maddi could wake up and see us." She pushes against my chest, but I don't loosen my hold.

"Maddi sleeps late. She always has. Even if she does wake up and come in here, we are both still dressed," I point out. I think this fact should help her relax, but she doesn't, not even a little. In fact, her body seems to get even tighter.

"How did I get in your bed?"

"I brought you in here," I say. Then I mutter, "Now go back to sleep."

"I can't sleep."

I hear the distress in her voice. "You can, or at least you could pretend since I'm comfortable."

"I think I should get up and take Merida out. She might need it . . . ," she tries.

"Merida is fine." I give her a squeeze. "Now sleep."

"I can't sleep."

"Try."

"You're being annoying."

"Sleep," I repeat, hearing her let out an annoyed or frustrated huff. I'm not sure which one.

"I can't believe you're holding me hostage in your bed."

I smile at that, then slide my hand from her back and down to her ass, pulling her against me. "If you were really my hostage, you'd be naked and tied up."

I feel her shiver as she breathes, "Holy cow."

"Sleep."

"Now I really won't be able to sleep," she grumbles. I chuckle. "Seriously."

"Try anyway," I command. She mutters something, trying to pull away one more time before giving up with another huff. I don't know how long it takes her to fall back asleep, but she does. When she does, so do I.

∼

"Yay, you slept over!"

As Maddi's happy voice greets my sleep-addled brain, I feel the bed shift. I blink one eye open, then the other.

Courtney takes Maddi's hand and leads her out of the room, talking to her quietly as they go. I roll to my back, then sit up, then stand. The girls are in the living room chatting quietly as I head for the bathroom, where I go through my morning routine. Once I'm done, I grab my sneakers from the bottom of my closet so I can put them on and take Merida for a quick walk. When I step out of the bedroom, I find Maddi putting on her shoes. She's still wearing her PJs, and Courtney is slipping on her flats.

"I'll take Merida out while you two figure out what we should do for breakfast," I offer, to save them the trouble.

"Lucas."

I focus on Courtney's face, and I can tell by her murderous expression that she's not happy about Maddi finding her in my bed this morning. I also don't care. Sometime between last night and this morning, I decided that she's going to be around a lot more. She will definitely make a habit of spending the night. She fits here with us, and I know she has to feel it, too.

Screw going too fast.

"If you don't feel like making something here, I'll pick up bagels while I'm out."

"Lucas—" she starts, but Maddi cuts in.

"I vote for bagels. Can I have a raisin one with cinnamon cream cheese, Daddy?"

"Sure, honey." My eyes go to Courtney. "What would you like?"

Letting out a long breath, she shakes her head. "I'll have a plain bagel with plain cream cheese."

I nod, then move to grab Merida's leash.

Courtney stops me, asking, "How are you going to pick up bagels if you have Merida with you?"

"I'll leave her outside."

"Outside?" Her eyes widen.

"Yeah, outside the shop. She'll be fine."

"Lucas, we just brought her home. We don't know if she will be okay tied up outside while you're inside and out of sight."

"She was all over the city with us yesterday," I remind her. Then I add, "We left her outside Starbucks while we went in to get drinks."

"But I was watching her through the window."

"I'll keep an eye on her."

"We should go with you. Or maybe I should go home for a bit and sho—"

"No!" Maddi cries. Courtney's head flies her way. "You can't go home."

"Sweetheart . . . ," Courtney says softly, only to be cut off again.

"I was hoping we could watch movies and spend the day together."

"I'd just go home to shower. I'll change and then come back, sweetie," Courtney says gently, grabbing Maddi's hand. "I'll come back."

"We can *all* go to your place, and then we can *all* come back here," Maddi suggests, sounding hopeful.

"I . . ." Courtney looks up at me.

"Works for me," I agree. I look at Maddi. "Go brush your teeth and get dressed. We'll go when you're ready."

"Okay!" She smiles, then runs out of the room with Merida following behind her.

"Lucas . . ." Courtney's tone is filled with warning.

When my eyes meet hers, I know that the expression she was wearing earlier *wasn't* murderous, because this one truly is. "This is too much too soon."

"It's not," I disagree with a shake of my head.

"Yes, it is. She could get confused and—"

"And what? You told me you're falling in love with her. She feels the same, and I know that I'm enjoying every single moment I have with you. This is good."

"This could end, and—"

"You're right. It could. We could figure out that we actually hate each other. Or I could get hit by a car going to work tomorrow, and this could all come to an end."

"Don't say that," she hisses, her face going pale.

I grab her hand and pull her against me, then drop my face close to hers. "Baby, the point is *anything* can happen, but I know I'd regret losing time with you more than I'd regret anything else. I like the way this feels. I like having you here with us. I might be wrong, but I think you like being here with us, too."

"I just . . . I just don't want anyone to get hurt." She drops her eyes from mine.

I give her a squeeze to get her attention.

"I know. I don't want that, either. But in life, if you try to guard against everything that might hurt you, you'll end up missing out and having regrets. I don't know what the future holds for us, but I do know that right now you and I are going to make out until Maddi comes rushing back in here. Then we're going to take Merida for a walk, stop to pick up bagels, and head to your place so you can shower and change. After you do that, we'll eat, take Merida for another walk, then spend the rest of the afternoon here on the couch watching movies. We can have dinner together. And tonight"—I drop my voice—"after Maddi goes to bed, you and I are going to make out some more before I will be forced to let you go so that you can go home to sleep. But I know I'll be wishing you were sleeping with me, because I really fucking liked holding you last night."

"Oh," she breathes, her eyes wide.

"Now are you ready for the first part of our day to start?"

"Maddi . . ."

"I'll hear her," I say, sliding my hand up her back to cup her head. I capture her hair in my grasp, then use it to tilt her head to the side right before my mouth hits hers. The moment our lips meet, her hands—which were resting on my waist—dig into my skin through my T-shirt. I lick across the seam of her lips, and she opens for me. I kiss her deeply, taking everything she's willing to give and then some. I only let up when I hear Maddi getting ready to rush into the room. I pull my mouth from hers and smile when I see the dazed look in her eyes.

"I'm ready!" Maddi cries on cue.

I laugh.

Courtney's fingers tense at my sides before she drops her fore-head to my chest and giggles. Hearing that carefree sound come from her, I wrap my arms around her in a hug and then kiss the top of her head.

"Get on your shoes, honey," I tell Maddi over the top of Courtney's head.

She nods with a bright smile before rushing to do as she was told.

"Please don't be too good to be true."

At Courtney's quietly spoken words, I look down at the top of her head. I rest my lips there, thinking the exact same thing about her.

Chapter 9

WARMTH

COURTNEY

Getting into the elevator at work, I check the time on my cell phone and smile when I see the image on the screen of Madeline laughing while Merida licks her face. I didn't even know that Madeline had gotten hold of my phone at some point yesterday until I went to call Lucas—to let him know I got home okay last night—and saw my new screensaver.

Glancing at the time, I see that I'm actually twenty minutes early. I get off the elevator and head down the carpeted hall toward the office I share with Abby. Before I even reach the door I spot her at her desk. I wonder how long she's been there. Ours is one of the largest corner offices on the floor. Abby's desk is in the back of the room, and is set up so she has a view out the floor-to-ceiling glass windows and the door. My desk faces the door so clients see me first. I doubt I would love sharing such a close space with anyone but Abby. She's always in a good mood unless she's not getting what she wants from a client's spouse—which does happen from time to time.

Not wanting to disturb Abby, who is on the phone, I go to my desk and quietly drop my bag, then pick up the notes that I left for myself on Friday.

"So how was your weekend?" Abby startles me, and I spin to face her.

"It was . . ." I try to think of the right words to use to describe how unbelievably perfect it was.

Yes, this whole thing is scary, but it feels good being with Lucas and Maddi.

"It was what?" Abby questions, having given up on waiting for me to find my words and answer.

"It was perfect, Abby. So perfect that it was a little scary."

I drop my notes on top of my desk, then head across the office toward the small kitchen, where there is already a pot of coffee brewing.

"Why is it scary?" she asks as I pour us each a cup.

I set her cup on her desk. "We basically spent the entire weekend together—Maddi, Lucas, and I. I even ended up spending the night at their place on Saturday after we adopted Merida," I say, knowing she knows who Merida is since I sent her a photo of her Saturday night after Maddi and I chose her name.

"You spent the night? Have you . . . ?"

"No." I shake my head. "I fell asleep reading to Madeline, and Lucas carried me to his bed. I didn't even wake up. When I *did* wake up, I tried to leave. He wouldn't let me."

"He wouldn't let you leave?" Her eyes are wide—not with worry, but with awe.

"No, he wouldn't."

"Wow," she breathes.

I can't help but smile, because it *was* "wow." I was a tad annoyed at him at the time for his high-handedness, but I really didn't want to leave, either. I liked him holding me. Not that I will ever admit that

95

I like his bossy side, since I'm pretty sure that should be considered a negative.

"Then you spent Sunday with them?"

"Yeah. Madeline didn't want me to leave. They ended up coming back to my place with me . . ." I look out the window behind her. "I think I'm falling in love with them *both*, which is insane."

"It's not insane if it feels right." Her quiet words pull my attention from the view.

"Yeah, but it is too soon after—"

"Stop." She cuts me off, her face and voice hard. "Tom and your past *do not* factor into this. You don't need to feel guilty about being happy, babe. You deserve to be happy. From what I can see, Lucas is making you feel that way. So why question it?"

"I know logically that you're right. I'm just worried that this is too good to be true."

"What does Lucas say? Does he think this is going too fast?"

"No. If anything, I think he wants it to move faster. He told me that he likes having me with him and Maddi. I think . . . I think he wanted me to stay last night. But . . ."

"Maybe you should stop listening to that voice in your head and start listening to him."

"It would be different if he didn't have a daughter and it was just him that I had to think about," I admit before taking a sip of coffee.

"Yeah, but he does have a daughter. I get the feeling that he likes having you around her and in their lives."

"I don't want her to get hurt if things don't work out between her dad and me."

I don't want to get hurt, either, though. I know losing Lucas would be hard, but I would also be losing Maddi. I don't know if my heart would be able to handle the loss of both of them.

"I'm sorry to say this, babe, but in life you can't protect children from everything. If things between you and Lucas don't work out, it's going to suck, but she's a kid. She will bounce back. So will Lucas, and so will you. I think you know that firsthand."

"I do," I agree with a heavy sigh.

"Don't run from this to protect yourself, because you'll actually end up causing yourself pain. Enjoy it, take it one day at a time, and see where it goes," she says.

I think about the weekend. I think about how happy I was with Lucas and Maddi, and then I think about the fact that I really want more weekends just like that.

"When did you join Team Lucas?"

She looks thoughtful for a moment before answering. "He's good for you. I really like how he looks at you."

"How he *looks* at me?" I frown, and she grins in return.

"Yeah. Like he wants to toss you over his shoulder and carry you away to his cave, where he will protect you with his life and give you everything you could ever want."

"He doesn't look at me like *that*," I say as my heart starts to pound against my rib cage.

"Yeah, babe. He does." She holds my gaze.

I lick my bottom lip, not sure what to do with that information. I only know that I like hearing it a lot. Maybe too much.

"We should get to work," I finally say.

Abby laughs. "Yeah, let's do that. Right after you tell me when you're seeing him again."

"I'm not sure," I admit.

Just then my cell beeps, so I make my way to my bag to grab it.

"He didn't make plans with you?" she asks.

I shrug. "We didn't make plans after last night, but I assume I'll see him at some point this week."

I look at my phone and see a message from Lucas on my screen. My stomach does a little dip as I read.

Maddi in her whirlwind morning decided we should have tacos tonight.

Is he telling me because he wants me to join them?
I really want to join him and Maddi for tacos.

I don't blame her. Tacos are awesome.

After I press "Send," I hold my breath. The little bubble appears on the screen, telling me he's already replying.

Does dinner at six work for you?

I reply yes immediately, then wonder if I should have waited for a few minutes. I instantly forget my doubt when I see his reply come through.

Good, baby, see you tonight. Have a good day.

"What is it?" Abby asks.
I lift my head after dropping my phone back into my bag.
"I'm having tacos with Lucas and Maddi *tonight*."
"That smile on your face right now is the reason I like him," Abby says.
I touch my lips with the tips of my fingers. I didn't even know I was smiling.

～

After knocking on Lucas's apartment door, I rub the top of Merida's head. She wiggles impatiently at my side. I don't know who's more excited to be here—me or her. As soon as I got off work, I went to the store to pick up stuff for dessert before I went home to change and pick her up. She was happy to see me, and I was happy to find out that she could be left alone and not destroy everything in sight. When I told her that we were going to see Maddi and Lucas, I swear she understood me. It was as if she couldn't wait to get out of the apartment.

"Hey, baby," Lucas greets me as soon as he opens the door.

I smile up at him. I don't know how it's possible to have missed him—it's really only been a few hours since I saw him last—but I have. Lucas always looks hot, and today he's wearing a dark-red button-down shirt with the sleeves rolled up to his elbows and a pair of gray dress slacks.

"Hey," I breathe against his lips as he brushes his mouth against mine. I feel him smile.

"Missed you." He kisses me again, and my stomach does a flip.

"Me too," I admit.

His smile broadens as he steps back to let me into the apartment. Taking Merida's leash from me, he unhooks her. I watch her run off toward Maddi's room and use her nose to push the door open and her way inside.

"How was your day?" I follow him toward the kitchen, where I can smell taco meat already cooking.

"Good. Or rather, it was good until I got a call this afternoon from Maddi's school." He picks up an open beer off the counter and takes a swig from the bottle as I set down the shopping bag and my purse.

"What happened?"

"She kicked some kid in the nuts. He had to go to the nurse, so Maddi has detention for two days."

"What?" I stare at him, sure I heard him wrong.

"I only kicked him because he tried to kiss me," Maddi says, defending herself as she comes out of her room carrying Merida. I fight back a smile as I watch her nose scrunch up in six-year-old annoyance. "I don't think I should have gotten in trouble for defending myself."

"I don't, either," Lucas grumbles, in a voice barely loud enough to hear.

My foot twitches to kick him.

"Boys are very sensitive in that area of their body, sweetheart. I know you were defending yourself, but you could have really hurt him," I say gently.

She looks down at Merida and frowns. "I said I was sorry when he started to cry."

I press my lips together and look down at my feet so that she doesn't see me trying not to smile. It's not funny, but at the same time it's a *little* funny.

"Do I still get to go to Grandma and Grandpa's this weekend?" she asks, sounding worried.

I look up at that piece of news.

"Yeah, honey," Lucas mutters. His eyes come to me, and my expression must give away my curiosity. "My parents are taking Maddi to the aquarium and zoo this weekend, since they are going to be out of town during her birthday."

"That sounds like fun." I look at Maddi, and I can see that her smile doesn't reach her eyes. I can tell she's upset that she got into trouble. Even though the kid probably deserved to be kicked, she's feeling a little guilty for hurting him. "So is Merida the only one who gets a Maddi hug?" I ask.

Her eyes light up. She comes to me, still holding Merida, and I wrap my arms around her and then kiss the side of her head. I don't care if I'm overstepping some hidden boundary. When I let her go, her smile seems more genuine. I smile back.

"I brought stuff to make dirt cups. Do you want to help me make them while your dad finishes dinner?"

"Dirt cups?" She giggles.

"It's not *really* dirt. It's chocolate pudding mixed with whipped cream topped with crushed Oreos and gummy worms."

"They sound yummy." Her eyes light up.

"They *are* yummy." I pull the stuff out of my shopping bag, then tip my head at Lucas when he sets a glass of wine near me on the counter.

The expression on his face is so warm that I feel that warmth wash through me and settle somewhere deep inside my soul where I didn't even know I was cold.

"Thanks," I whisper.

He dips his chin, then kisses the side of my head.

"So what do we do first?" Maddi asks.

I look down at the beautiful girl who has taken a part of my heart and say softly, "First we wash our hands. Then we make dirt."

Feeling Lucas's lips touch the top of my head, I look into his beautiful eyes.

After the delicious tacos, he, Maddi, and I watch a couple of her shows on TV. Then it's time for her to shower and get into bed. Like on Saturday, she asks me to read her a book, and, like on Saturday, my heart melts when she curls up against me while I read to her. *The Princess and the Pea*, again. I don't fall asleep this time, but she does before I make it even halfway through the story. I lie there with her for a long time, soaking in the feeling of holding her before I get out of bed, kiss her head, and turn out her light.

When I turn to leave the room, I find Lucas standing in the doorway with the same warm expression on his face that he had earlier—a look I try to memorize as he holds out his hand toward me. When his fingers wrap around mine, I let him lead me to the couch. He settles me against him, wrapping his arm around my shoulder. His hand rests on my hip, and his fingers slide under my top to run softly against my skin.

"Thank you." His softly spoken words pull me from my thoughts, and I study his expression.

"For what?" I ask, not understanding the look in his eyes.

"Maddi was upset when she got home from school. When she gets into trouble, she always closes down. I expected her to stay locked in her head for a few days, but within a few minutes of you being here she was back to being herself. Thank you for that."

"I think she felt bad for hurting the boy."

"She shouldn't feel bad. He shouldn't have kissed her."

"Honey . . ." I turn so my front is to the back of the couch. Once I'm facing him, I rest my hands against his chest. "You're right. He shouldn't have kissed her, but she shouldn't have hurt him."

"Yes, she should have," he growls.

Seeing the look on his face, I realize what I'm doing. I press my lips together to keep my mouth shut. It's not my place to argue with him about how Madeline should or shouldn't act.

"What's that?" His brows pull together as his eyes scan my face.

"What?"

"You. What's that look that you just got? One second you're ready to battle with me, and the next you're pressing your lips together like you're attempting to keep quiet."

"Nothing." I turn back to face the TV, which is now playing the news.

"Talk to me," he demands, putting his hand under my jaw to force me to look at him.

"It's nothing. It's not my place."

"Not your place." His eyes turn kind of scary, and I try not to flinch. "You're in our lives. In my life. I want to hear what you have to say. I want to know what you think."

"I . . . I'm . . . It's not my place to argue with you about Madeline."

"Pardon?"

Even though I can hear the slight warning in his tone, I still say softly, "I'm not her mom. We are all just getting to know each other, so I don't think it's my place to tell you how Maddi should or shouldn't act."

"When *does* it become your place?"

"I don't know. I don't know how these things work," I say quietly.

His jaw twitches. "Maddi was going to freak Sunday when you said you were going home. She didn't want to miss out on time with you. Twice now you've lain in bed with her and read her a bedtime story, shared something with her that has only been mine since the day she was born. She never even asked her mom to read to her. We like you being here, and I plan on you being here for a long fucking time. So tell me, baby, when will it be your place to give me your opinion?"

He noticed that Maddi didn't want me to leave Sunday? Holy cow, she's never even asked her mom to read to her at night?

"I can tell by your expression that you don't get what I'm saying, so let me make it clear. I want you in my life. I want you in Maddi's life. I want to know how you feel. I want to hear your opinion, even if I don't agree with you."

"Okay," I agree.

My heart beats so hard that it feels like it might explode out of my chest. If I had any doubt before about what he wanted, I don't now.

"Okay." He shakes his head, then his eyes go to the television.

I give his waist a squeeze and wait for him to look at me before I say quietly, "I'm proud of her for sticking up for herself, but she shouldn't have kicked him so hard that he had to go to the nurse's office."

His lips twitch into a smile, then he kisses the top of my head and mumbles, "Yeah, but I bet he'll think twice before he kisses another girl."

"This is true," I mutter back.

He laughs hard, then his laughing mouth is covering mine and he's laying me back against the couch and covering me with his body. When his tongue slips between my lips, I lose myself in his kiss.

"Heads up," he states when he pulls his mouth from mine minutes, or maybe hours, later. "You're staying here with me from Friday to Sunday, so you might want to plan for that."

"What?" I blink and attempt to focus on him and not my over-heated body or the way my blood seems to be singing through my veins.

"Or we'll stay at your place. Either way, don't plan on doing anything this weekend, because I plan on keeping us both busy."

"Oh . . . ," I breathe.

"Oh yeah." He smiles once more before his mouth covers mine again.

I lose myself in his kisses.

Chapter 10

THE EX IS BACK IN TOWN

COURTNEY

"What do you think?" I turn to face Merida, who's sprawled out on my bed with her legs up in the air and her head tipped back in my direction. She rolls to her stomach and sits up, her head tilting one way, then the other. "Do you think it's too much?" I ask, even knowing she has no idea what I'm saying. "It's probably too much."

I look down at myself, then turn to face the mirror. When Lucas told me last night that we would be spending the weekend together, I knew what that meant. I also know that I'll be ready for everything that will hopefully happen between us. More than ready.

Okay, mostly ready and kind of freaking out.

When I went through my lingerie drawer this morning, I found I own not one sexy piece of underwear. I don't even own a nightgown, let alone a sexy nightie. I tossed everything when my marriage came to an end. After Tom I got rid of all my stuff, not wanting the memories they held. I bought all new undergarments in soft cotton. Cotton is awesome, but it's not sexy—or at least the stuff I have isn't sexy. I need something to wear for Lucas that will hopefully say to him that I'm ready for the step we're taking—and looking forward to it.

When I got to work this morning, I told Abby about my dilemma. She promised she knew just the place to take me.

I bite my lip and scan my reflection. The woman at the exclusive boutique in SoHo where Abby took me picked this bodysuit when Abby told her I was looking for something special to wear for my man. The idea of Lucas being "my man"—and the price of the scrap of fabric—just about gave me a heart attack, but the saleswoman told me to trust her.

Looking at myself, I have to admit that it was worth every penny. The silky-soft, see-through black mesh is beautiful, and the corded panels that dart out from under my breasts and end at the tops of my hips enhance my waist, making it look like I have an hourglass figure. There is lace both at the curve of my hips and over my breasts, and the underwire gives me amazing cleavage, which is even more dramatic because of the thin black straps that stretch over my shoulders. Turning, I look at my bottom and the almost nonexistent material covering it.

"It might be too much, but this is seriously sexy," I whisper to myself.

I carefully slip out of the bodysuit and fold it up, then wrap myself in my robe. I go to my dresser and pull out all my old cotton panties and bras, replacing them with my new stuff.

My cell phone rings. I sigh when I see who's calling.

"Hello?" I answer after putting my phone to my ear.

"Courtney!" Lorie's voice greets me as I take a seat on the bed. Merida comes to sit on my lap. "You haven't called me back since our last text."

"I know. I'm sorry." I run my fingers through Merida's fur. "How are you?"

"I've . . . Well . . . I've been okay, but I've been worried about you."

I lean back against my headboard and close my eyes. "I should have called you and told you I was okay. Things have just been busy around here with my new job, the house, and getting settled."

"I understand." The strain in her voice eats at my stomach. "I miss you."

"Me too." It's not a lie. I *do* miss her, but things are different now.

"I'll be in the city Friday to do some shopping. I was hoping that we could meet up for dinner? Maybe you can show me your house?"

"I'd love to have dinner." My stomach tightens with anxiety as I lie. "I'm not sure you'll be able to see the house, since it's still under construction."

"That's okay." She inhales. "I . . . I know you probably don't want to hear about this, but Tom has moved into his own place and is going for custody. Things . . . Well . . . things haven't been good between him and—"

"Lorie." I stop her. "I don't want to cut you off, but I honestly don't want to hear about Tom. I know he's your son, but—"

"Of course. Sorry, I just—"

"It's okay. I . . ." I rub my lips together. "I'm trying to focus on my future."

"Are you happy?"

"Yes." My answer is immediate. I *am* happy, maybe even happier than I have ever been in my life.

"I should let you go. I'll message you soon, and we'll figure out a time to meet."

"Okay," I start to agree, but the phone call ends before I can get the word out.

When I pull my phone from my ear, I let out a long breath and close my eyes. I probably shouldn't have agreed to see her. I don't think this situation is any easier for her, and I wonder if I'm not hurting her more by trying to keep her in my life.

Merida nudges my stomach with her nose. I look down at her. "Well, girl, the good news is that no matter what happens with Lorie, I have a whole weekend with Lucas to look forward to."

She groans her agreement, then licks my face before moving to lie down at the end of the bed.

I get up and go to the bathroom, take a shower, put on one of my new nighties, and get into bed. I text Lucas to let him know I'm turning in and smile when I see he's already messaged me.

Maddi and I missed you tonight.

I missed him and Madeline, too. But I had promised Abby I would have dinner with her after shopping, and I didn't want to cancel. It was also nice to catch up with her, even though I see her every day. We don't always have time to just chat.

Missed you both, too. Dinner tomorrow night? I'll cook.

I send the text and try to wait for his reply, but before long my eyes grow too heavy to keep open.

∼

The next morning, I open up my text messages and fight back a frown when I see that Lucas still hasn't replied. I tuck my cell phone back in my bag and try to forget about it. I figure he probably just fell asleep last night and then spent the morning running around getting Madeline ready for school.

When I get into the office, I don't even have a chance to set down my purse before Abby tells me that we have a meeting with a new client.

∼

Sitting down to lunch with Abby later in the afternoon, I pull out my phone for the first time since the morning. Relief washes over me when I see that Lucas has called twice and texted a few times. My heart sinks and my stomach twists when I read his texts, though.

Sorry I didn't message you back last night, Eva showed up and ended up staying over.

Eva as in Madeline's mom, his ex-wife?

She left her boyfriend and is in the city, planning to stay with a friend of hers that lives here.

She wants to see Maddi tonight, so we'll have to make plans for later this week.

I'm sorry, baby, I'll call you this afternoon when I get a chance.

"What's going on?" Abby's voice pulls my attention away from my phone.

I try to mask my emotions so she won't read how upset I am. Lucas has never given me a reason not to trust him, but Tom never gave me a reason not to trust him, either. I know that Lucas is not Tom, but I also know that it would cut me deeply if something like that ever happened between us. As much as I thought I loved Tom, I'm realizing now that I might have just latched on to him because it was comfortable.

"It's nothing." I shrug and tuck my cell back into my bag without sending a reply to Lucas.

"Your face is saying something else."

Thankfully, the waiter comes over to ask for our drink orders, giving me a few minutes to get my emotions under control. When he leaves, I study the menu like whatever I select will be cooked for us tableside by Gordon Ramsay himself.

"Okay, seriously. What's going on?" Abby demands.

Apparently, I should never, ever play poker.

"Lucas's ex-wife broke up with her man and stayed with Lucas and Maddi last night. She is also having dinner with Lucas and Maddi tonight. She's moving back to the city and is going to be staying with a friend of hers."

I bite my lip when I finish speaking, wishing I had a glass of wine to wash down the bitterness in my throat.

"Wait. What?" Abby's eyes grow concerned.

I lean back against the leather booth. "Like I said. Lucas's ex is in the city, and Lucas and Maddi are having dinner with her tonight."

"What the actual fuck?" she whispers.

I'm glad she's using her "inside voice," because the restaurant is really nice and they would probably frown upon her using that language in here.

Not having an immediate response, I shrug. I look toward the bar and mutter, "Is it too early to start drinking?"

"Babe," Abby calls to get my attention. My eyes move from the bar to her. "Please don't worry about this."

"I'm not." The lie tastes bitter as it leaves my mouth. "She's Maddi's mom. I'm glad she wants to spend time with her daughter," I lie again.

Eva and Lucas have history. They have a daughter together. They are connected. They will *always* be connected because of Maddi. If I'm honest, I'm jealous—and a little worried. .

What if she wants him back? What if he's willing to try to work things out because of Maddi?

Shaking her head, Abby sighs, looks across the room, and lifts her chin. A moment later the waiter appears. When he asks what she needs, she orders us a bottle of wine. We drink a lot—so much that I'm drunk by the time lunch is over. I don't go back to the office. Instead, Abby gets us a cab and takes me home before walking Merida. I don't remember much besides getting into bed and falling asleep with Abby running her fingers through my hair and telling me everything will be all right.

～

My head is pounding when I wake up. It takes me a minute to realize that the pounding is only getting worse—because there is a loud banging coming from my front door. I get out of bed and head across my apartment. When I open the door, my stomach turns with nausea.

"What the fuck?" Lucas barks, pushing his way past me and slamming the door closed. Merida barks once, then twice, but stops when his head swings to her. He pins her with a look that says, "Stop," so she does. And sits.

"Lucas?" I look from him to the door.

"Yeah, Lucas. The guy you're seeing? The one who's been calling you all fucking day and is worried sick because you haven't answered or returned any of his messages? Glad to know you remember me."

"I . . ."

"What the fuck?" he questions again before I can get a word in edgewise.

"I . . . I fell asleep." I leave out the part about drinking in an attempt to get the thought of him and his ex sleeping under the same roof and having dinner together out of my head.

"It's not even six. Are you sick?"

"No . . ." I shake my head, then ask, "Where's Maddi?"

"With my brother and his wife. I've been worried about you, so I asked them to keep an eye on her while I came to see if you were okay."

"What?"

"Did you miss the part where I said I've been calling you all day, and you haven't called me back or replied to any of my messages?"

"I . . ." I wrap my arms around my waist. "Well, I know you're having dinner with Eva and Maddi tonight. I didn't want to disturb you."

"Disturb me?" His eyes narrow.

"Yeah," I whisper.

Suddenly his expression changes, and his features soften along with his voice as he says, "Talk to me."

"What?"

I take a step back without thinking, then stop myself before I take another. I don't want to tell him that in my mind he and his ex are going to work things out and I will be left alone again.

"Talk about what?" I play dumb.

"Are you worried about me having dinner with Eva?"

God, even thinking about him and her in the same room makes me want to be sick, but I can't let him know that.

"No," I lie once more.

"Good. You shouldn't be. She and I are done. We were done probably before we even started, baby." He takes a step toward me but stops before he's within touching distance. "She stayed last night because she couldn't get ahold of her friend. The only reason I agreed to dinner is because Maddi hasn't been around Eva much, and I don't want her freaked out now that her mother has moved back to the city."

I close my eyes and drop my head forward.

Of course he would want to make sure that Maddi is okay. Of course he would insist on seeing to that himself.

"I'm an idiot."

"You're not an idiot. I don't think I'd be any happier about the idea of you spending time with your ex-husband."

I lift my head and look into his eyes.

"Is that why you haven't answered my calls?"

"I had a drink at lunch."

He raises a brow.

"Abby and I shared a bottle of wine. Well, Abby had one glass from the bottle, I had the rest. When you didn't text me back this morning, and then when I saw your message . . ." My words taper off.

"You were worried?"

"Yes. I know, it's stupid."

"It's not stupid, but I'm not your ex, baby. I wouldn't cheat on you. I understand that it's going to take some time for you to realize that, but I need you to try to trust me."

"I'm trying," I say quietly. "I just . . . Well, I just like you a lot, and it scares me. What Tom did hurt, but with you I—"

My words end on a gasp, because the next thing I know I'm in his arms and his mouth is crushed against mine for a hard, possessive kiss.

"I won't *ever* do that to you," he states when he pulls his mouth from mine. He keeps his face so close that he's all I can see. "He's a coward. He should have ended things with you. He should have been a man and told you that he wanted something different before he stepped out on you." His hold on me tightens. "I don't know where we are going, but I *do* know that I would never hurt you like that. I would never step out on you the way he did."

"I believe you," I say, looking into his eyes. "I'm sorry about not answering your calls or messaging you back."

"I want to say it's okay, but it's not. I've been a mess all day, worried about you."

He's been a mess, worried about me?

My body melts deeper into his. He says, "I've never felt this way before." His hand wraps around the side of my neck, then his fingers slide up into my hair. "I didn't like not being able to reach you. The idea of—" He shakes his head, cutting off his own words. "Just, from now on, if you have concerns or worries, promise you'll talk to me before you cut me out?"

"Okay," I agree, untangling my fingers from his shirt and running my palms up his stomach to rest against his hard chest. "I'm sorry for making you worry."

"It's all right as long as it doesn't happen again." He lowers his head, and his lips touch mine softly. "You okay now?"

"Yes." I slide my hands up to his shoulders, then ask, "Is Maddi happy that her mom's here?"

"She was a little freaked when she woke up this morning and Eva was there. She brought you up when Eva told her about dinner tonight. She asked if you would be coming, then got upset when I told her no."

My sweet girl. God, I love her.

"She's upset that she hasn't seen you or Merida for two nights."

"Maybe we can have dinner tomorrow?" I suggest hopefully.

"Yeah, and I'm going to hold you to your promise of cooking for us."

"I didn't promise I would cook."

"Your last message said you'd cook."

"That was before."

"So you're telling me that you *won't* cook for me and my girl?"

"I'll cook for me and Maddi. *You* can order a pizza or something," I tease.

He grins. "I miss you. Even here, with you in my arms, I miss you because I know I have to go and I can't take you with me."

His words make my heart turn over in my chest and my stomach melt.

"I feel the same way," I tell him.

His eyes run over my face. "I'll see you tomorrow evening, but I expect you to answer when I call you tonight."

"I'll answer," I agree, getting on my tiptoes and pressing my mouth to his.

I start the kiss but he takes over, sliding his arm around my waist and twisting his hand in my hair to move my head from side to side as his tongue slips between my lips. When he pulls his mouth away, I'm panting and my whole body is buzzing from head to toe.

"I'm really looking forward to this weekend," he growls, nipping my bottom lip.

I whimper in response.

When his hold on me loosens, I let him lead me to the door with his arm around my waist. He opens the door and kisses me one more time before leaving. I lean against the doorjamb in a daze, watching him go. He turns to look at me over his shoulder, and his eyes roam over me.

"By the way, I really like your nightie." He winks, and I feel my eyes widen.

I look down and feel myself blush. I forgot that I'd put on one of my new nighties before I got into bed. This one is baby blue, with dark-blue lace at the edges of my breasts and thighs.

I shut the door most of the way, and he laughs. I poke just my head out. "If you like this, wait until you see what I bought especially for you . . ."

I can't believe I just said that.

My face heats.

He turns to face me but continues walking backward. "Baby, believe me when I say I won't give a fuck what you have on, because I'm really fucking looking forward to seeing all of you."

His words cause my legs to shake and my body to tingle in places it hasn't ever tingled before. Even though he *says* he won't care, I guarantee that he will when he sees me in the bodysuit.

With that thought in my head, I smile and shut the door.

Chapter 11

Unexpected Company

Lucas

"Hey," Eva says with a smile when she spots Maddi and me.

I lift my chin in greeting, and Maddi's hand tightens around mine. A second later, my stomach clenches—not in the way it does when I'm with Courtney, but like I'm going to be sick.

Eva closes the distance between us. Instead of greeting her daughter like she should, she rests her hand against my chest and tries to kiss my cheek.

What the actual fuck?

I lean back before she can make contact and send her a warning look. Her happy expression falters for a second, then she schools her features and leans down, touching her lips to the top of Maddi's head and saying a soft hello.

When she stands to her full height again, she says, "I put our name on the waiting list. They said it will be about ten minutes before we have a table."

"That's fine," I say, wishing I didn't have to be here. I wish that she weren't the mother of my child and that I could write her out of my life. Unfortunately, that's not possible. Until Maddi is eighteen, I will have to deal with Eva on some level. Last night, when she showed up at the apartment and said she couldn't get ahold of her best friend, Heather, and needed a place to stay for the night, I wanted to turn her away. As much as I wanted to slam the door in her face, I couldn't. Even if she's not really a mother to Maddi, she's still her mom.

"How was school, Madeline?" she asks.

I look down at Maddi and notice that her face is lowered toward the ground and her shoulders are tight with tension.

"It was okay." She shrugs, keeping her head down.

"You should look at the person you're speaking to," Eva scolds.

My free hand clenches into a fist. "Eva . . ." I growl her name, and she looks up at me.

"What?"

"Don't." That one word rumbles out of me in warning.

"She should—"

I cut her off. "I said *don't.*"

Her eyes narrow. I put up with her bullshit when we were married because I didn't want to rock our boat any more than it was already rocking, but that was then and this is now. I hate how she talks to Maddi. I hate the way she makes my baby's shoulders slump and her eyes fill with sadness. I know it's because she thinks she will never be able to please her mother.

"Fine," she huffs out.

My jaw tightens. Our name is called—or rather, *my* last name is called. A name that Eva stopped using when we got divorced. Why she might have used it on the list is something I try not to think about.

At the booth we're led to, I place Maddi next to me and leave Eva on the other side, alone. When the waiter comes over a few minutes later to take our orders, I ask for a burger and fries for myself and a grilled cheese and fries for Maddi—something that I can tell Eva doesn't like, because the look on her face makes it clear. Thankfully, she keeps her mouth closed about me not forcing Maddi to eat some kind of vegetable with her meal.

"Are you excited for your birthday?" Eva asks halfway through what turns out to be a mostly silent dinner.

Maddi's face lights up with excitement for the first time, and she nods. "Yes. Aunt Libby told me that she is going to decorate with unicorns, and Daddy ordered me a unicorn cake for the party."

"I can't wait to see it," Eva says.

I feel my muscles bunch.

"Me either," Maddi nods. Then, looking up at me, she asks, "Is Courtney coming?"

Looking at my baby girl, I smile and nod. I haven't asked Courtney, but I have no doubt that she will want to be there for the party.

"Yay!" Maddi grins, and I touch my lips to her head while wrapping my arm around her shoulder.

"Your new girlfriend is coming to our daughter's birthday party?" Eva asks.

"Yeah."

"Do you think that's smart? Didn't you just start seeing her?" I can hear the annoyance in her voice and see it in her eyes.

"Don't go there, Eva."

"I just don't think it's smart to have a person in her life that you hardly know."

"Do *not* go there," I repeat.

She sits back, crossing her arms over her chest. "She's my daughter, too. I have the right to know who you have around her."

"We are *not* doing this right now," I state, my voice hard. No way is she going to tell me whom I can and can't see or whom I can and can't have around our daughter, not when she's barely been around the last couple of years.

"I *want* Courtney at my party." Maddi cuts into my stare-down with Eva, and I look at my girl.

"She'll be there, honey."

"Do you think Merida can come, too?"

"Merida?" Eva asks.

"The dog we adopted last weekend," Maddi answers.

Eva looks startled by the news. When we were married, she wanted us to get a dog, but I refused. It wasn't that I didn't want a dog, but my plate was full already, and I knew that taking care of any animal we got would fall to me. Maddi was too young to help, and Eva was too selfish to care for anyone or anything but herself.

"I don't think dogs are allowed, but I'm sure you'll see Merida when the party's over. You'll also see her tomorrow, since Courtney is coming over to cook dinner for us," I say.

She smiles.

"I might need somewhere to stay for a couple more days," Eva says.

I look at her, feeling my jaw twitch and tighten.

"I thought you were staying with Heather?"

"I am, but she only has one extra room, and her parents are in town for a few days."

"I'm sure she has a couch."

"She does, but so do you. I'd like to spend time with my daughter."

"You know you're always welcome to see Maddi, but last night was a one-time thing," I state.

She presses her lips together.

No way is she staying the night again.

"Can I go to the bathroom, Daddy?" Maddi asks.

I look at the bathroom; it's directly across the room from us. Knowing I will be able to see her go and come back, I nod and slide out of the booth. I watch her go and disappear behind the door, then take a seat while keeping my eyes on the closed door.

"I think we should talk about us," Eva says.

I don't look at her. I should have known by the way she's been acting that she thinks I'll take her back.

No way is that happening.

"There is no 'us' to talk about."

"Lucas, I've had a lot of time to think. I know I didn't appreciate you like I should have. I'm just asking for a chance to prove I've changed, that we can make this work."

"That's never going to happen." I glance at her. "You want a relationship with your daughter, I'm all for that. You're her mom. She needs you in her life. But there's nothing for us to go back to."

"Is this because of the woman you're seeing?"

"Partly. I won't let you come between what Courtney and I are building, but even if I didn't have her, I wouldn't go there with you."

"Really?" she asks snidely, like she can't believe anyone wouldn't want her.

As Maddi heads back to the table, I stand and look down at Eva, saying quietly, "Work on your relationship with your daughter, Eva. She's growing up and doing it fast. You've already missed out on a lot." I stop speaking when Maddi reaches the table, then sit down after she slides into the booth.

Through the rest of dinner, Eva is quiet. I can tell she's not happy, but I don't give a fuck. She's in my past, and I plan on keeping her there. When we leave the restaurant, she kisses Maddi's head and tells her goodbye, then tries to give me a hug. I back away from her before she even gets close. From the look in her eyes, I can tell she's taking my rejection as a challenge.

~

"Daddy, why doesn't my mom love me?" Maddi's softly spoken question as I tuck her into bed later that night makes my chest tighten and anger flow through my veins.

I always knew that she wondered why she didn't have a typical mother-daughter relationship with Eva, but I had no idea that she thought her mom didn't love her.

"She does love you." I lean into her, resting my hand against her soft cheek.

"I don't think she does. I wish Courtney was my mom," she whispers back.

Looking into my baby girl's eyes, I vow that I won't let Eva cause any more damage than she already has. I need to do a better job of protecting Maddi from her.

"Your mom does love you. Never doubt that." I lean in and kiss her forehead, holding my lips there and wishing that I could change her mom. Wishing I could make Eva see what she's doing to our daughter. "Are you ready for a story?" I scoot her over and lie down next to her.

"I wish Courtney was here to read to me," she says, cuddling into me. My chest tightens even further.

"She'll be here to read to you tomorrow," I promise her.

I love that my baby is falling for the woman I'm falling in love with—a woman I know is worthy of that love. The differences between Courtney and Eva are glaringly obvious, especially when it comes to how they interact with Maddi.

When I finally get into my bed, I call Courtney and tell her about dinner. I tell her about the looks from Eva and the comments. I want to be honest with her, but I also want to warn her. I listen to her soft voice telling me she's sorry. The anger I was holding on to vanishes, and I know that, with her, it will always be like that. She soothes me, brings me peace and comfort when I need it most. I love my daughter with everything I am, but I wonder what it would have been like if I had met Courtney first.

"Oh no." I hear Courtney say this from the kitchen, where she and Maddi have been making dinner.

I put down the plans I've been working on at my drawing table and head that way, noticing that both girls are now quiet. They are *never* quiet. Or I should say Maddi is never quiet when Courtney is around. Since the moment Courtney and Merida got here, Maddi has been talking a mile a minute about school, her party, and the boy she kicked in the nuts—whom she now apparently has a crush on, though I've been ignoring that last part for the sake of my own sanity.

"Are they supposed to be black like that?" Maddi's worried voice fills the silence as the smell of smoke fills the air.

I make my way around the high counter that divides the kitchen from the living room, then stop. Courtney has the oven door open. Smoke is billowing out, and Maddi is peeking over her shoulder, trying to look into the oven.

"I don't think so." Courtney coughs, waving the oven mitt in front of her face.

I put Maddi behind me, then move Courtney aside. I take the oven mitts from her. I pull the pan out of the oven and set it on top of the stove, then hit the vent for the fan to help clear the air.

"You're right. I don't think they are supposed to be black like that," Maddi mumbles.

I chuckle while Courtney giggles.

"I think you're right, sweetheart." Courtney giggles harder, and I smile down at her as I look at the salmon she was cooking.

They're black and burned to a crisp. There is no salvaging it.

"Looks like I'm going to be ordering pizza after all," I say.

Courtney looks up and grins at me.

Yes, I'm falling head over heels in love with her. Or maybe I've already fallen.

"Sorry, the directions said to bake the salmon steaks, then to turn on the broiler to brown the top. I wasn't watching and lost track of time." She bites her lip, then looks down at the fish. "The green beans, couscous, and salad are still okay. Do you have some kind of meat we can defrost and cook?"

"The only thing we have in the freezer is ice cream and popsicles," Maddi informs us, then smiles. "We could have the apple pie you brought and ice cream for dinner?"

"Nice try, kid." I shake my head at her, and she shrugs as if to say it was worth a shot.

"I can run to the store and pick up a rotisserie chicken," Courtney suggests, getting the garbage can and tossing the fish away.

"I'll run to the store and take that out on my way," I say, taking the bag out of the trash. "Do we need anything else?"

"Not that I know of," Courtney says. She looks at Maddi, who shakes her head.

"All right. I'll be back in just a few." I kiss Courtney on the lips, then I kiss the top of Maddi's head. I grab my wallet off the end of the counter and head out the door. When I make it downstairs, I toss the garbage bag into the trash and then head for the store.

It takes me less than thirty minutes to make it through the store and get back home, but the moment I walk through the door I know something is off from the tension that seems to have filled the air.

The problem is sitting at the island, with what looks like a glass of wine in front of her. My body goes rigid.

"Hey, Lucas." Eva smiles at me with red lips. Her hair is done up, and the dress she's wearing barely covers her breasts and her crotch.

I don't acknowledge her. I look into the kitchen and see Courtney standing so close to Maddi you'd think she was attempting to fuse herself to her side.

"You girls okay?" I ask in a low tone.

Courtney nods and attempts to smile, but I can tell it's forced.

I look at Eva. "What are you doing here?"

"I wanted to come see Maddi." I look at the wine in front of her. "Your girlfriend offered me a glass." She smiles.

"Hey, Lucas." I turn and see Heather coming out of the bathroom. She's wearing something similar to the outfit that Eva has on.

"Heather." My jaw clenches. I don't even want to know what these two have been up to while I've been gone.

"I should take Merida out before we have dinner," Courtney says, cutting through the silence.

"I'll go with you." Maddi looks up at Courtney.

"I came to see you, Madeline," Eva says.

I know it's bullshit. She knew Courtney, Maddi, and I were having dinner tonight. She decided to stop by to stir up drama.

"You should stay and visit with your mom, sweetheart. I'll be right back," Courtney says softly.

I see Eva bristle. I follow Courtney to the door and watch her put the leash on Merida's collar. I open the door and step out with her, closing the door behind me.

"I'm sorry, baby. When you get back, they won't be here."

"It's okay," she says, not looking at me.

I wonder if Eva said something awful to her.

"Baby?" I wrap my hand around her jaw and lift until her eyes meet mine. "When you get back, they won't be here," I repeat.

I watch her chest rise and fall as she takes a deep breath.

"Okay."

"Okay." I press a kiss to her lips. "Don't stay gone too long."

"So I shouldn't get in a cab and go home? Or kidnap Maddi and run away with her?"

"Unless you're taking me with you, no." I rub my thumb across her bottom lip. "Come back soon."

She nods, and I kiss her once more. Then I let her go and watch her disappear down the steps. When she's gone, I pull in a breath to get my anger in check. I open the door to the apartment. Maddi is nowhere in sight, and her bedroom door is closed—letting me know she's hiding. Heather and Eva are both sitting at the island.

"She's cute," Eva says as I shut the door. "A little fat, but cute."

Courtney is not fat, she's perfect.

"You ever call her fat again, we're going to have more problems than we already have. You need to leave. Now."

"I thought you said I could spend time with Maddi."

"Maddi is hiding in her room to get *away* from you. You're not here to spend time with her, you're here to try and start shit."

"That's ridicul—"

"Don't." I lift my hand. "Don't push me, Eva. You need to leave."

"She just wants to spend time with Madeline," Heather says.

My eyes move to her, briefly.

"Leave."

"You said any—"

"That doesn't mean you get to stop by when you know we have plans. That means you send me a message and I will work a time out with you so you can spend time with her."

"She's my daughter."

"Then act like her mother, Eva. For fuck's sake. She's *hiding* in her room so she doesn't have to be around you. *You* did that. By coming here. She probably understands why you're really here."

"I didn't do anything."

"I'm not going to ask you again." I move to the door and open it.

"Let's go," Heather says.

Eva slides off the stool, glaring at me.

"I'm going to talk to a lawyer," Eva says, stopping in front of me.

"Do what you have to do, Eva. But just know I won't lose my daughter without a fight—and I will fight until I die to keep her with me, where she belongs."

She huffs but walks out, Heather pushing her along. I hear the sound of a dog collar clinking and turn, expecting to see Courtney and

Merida. Instead I see Fawn and Muffin coming up the stairs—with Courtney and Merida right behind them.

"Is everything okay?" Fawn asks, her eyes moving over both Heather and Eva.

"Everything is fucking wonderful," Eva snaps as she passes Fawn to head down the steps.

I can tell by Courtney's facial expression that Eva's giving her a dirty look.

"Well, I can't say I've missed *her* much," Fawn murmurs when she's close.

I don't take my eyes from Courtney. I reach out to her and take her hand when she's within reach. "You okay?"

"I think your ex is worse than mine, and I didn't think that was possible." Her eyes drop to my side, and I see her face soften at Maddi, who must have heard her mom leave and come out of hiding. "You okay, sweetheart?"

"Yes," Maddi says, picking up Merida and taking her over to Muffin, who greets the smaller dog by licking her face.

"Did you two meet?" I look between Courtney and Fawn.

"Yeah, we met outside when Muffin mowed down her dog. I figured out she was yours when she told me her dog's name. She told me Eva was over, so I told her she could come hang with me until it was safe to go back to your place." She looks at Courtney. "Maddi hasn't stopped talking about either of you."

"Where's Levi?" I ask.

Fawn looks at me. "Working. He has a case he's trying to close."

"We were just getting ready to have dinner. Would you like to join us?" Courtney asks.

"I . . ."

"We have plenty. Or . . ." Courtney looks at me and asks, "Did you get the chicken?"

"I did." I give her hand a squeeze.

"We have plenty." She looks at Fawn again. "I was going to make salmon, but there was an accident. So Lucas went out and picked up a rotisserie chicken from the store."

"Are you sure you don't mind?"

"Of course not." Courtney smiles at her, then turns for the apartment and walks in through the still-open door, taking me with her since she hasn't let go of my hand.

"What kind of 'accident' did you have with the salmon?" Fawn asks, following us inside with Muffin. Maddi's still carrying Merida.

"I put it to broil and burned it." Courtney shrugs, and Fawn laughs.

"I can't cook. I don't even know what broiling is. Thank god my husband knows his way around the kitchen, or we would starve." She takes a seat on one of the barstools.

"I can normally cook, or at least follow directions. But I wasn't paying attention this time." Courtney lets me go and unpacks the chicken, then moves around the kitchen getting plates and things out.

After I get everyone settled with drinks, I lean against the counter while listening to her and Fawn chat. My mom will love Courtney—I know that without a doubt. I also know my other two sisters-in-law will go crazy once they meet her. For the last year they have been trying to set me up with random women they know from the city. I never took them up on any of their offers, but that never stopped them from trying. They hated Eva, too—my whole family hated her and didn't understand why I was with her, aside from Maddi.

Throughout dinner I listen to Maddi, Fawn, and Courtney talk. I chime in every once in a while, but mostly I try to block out what they are talking about because they seem to spend most of dinner talking about the boy Maddi has a crush on. When dinner is done, we have the apple pie Courtney brought with her. Before long, Fawn says she has to get home and grade some papers for school in the morning. She gives Maddi and Courtney hugs before she heads across the hall to the apartment she shares with my brother—an apartment they will be moving out of soon, since Fawn is pregnant and they'll need a bigger place. Fawn doesn't know I know she's pregnant. Levi was supposed to keep things quiet for a few more weeks, but he was too excited to keep the news to himself. I'm happy for him and Fawn. They're good together, and they are going to be great parents.

Once I usher Maddi into the shower, I head to the kitchen. Courtney is cleaning up the rest of the dishes. I wrap my arms around her waist and rest my chin on her shoulder.

"Fawn loves you," I say.

She turns her head to look at me. "She's really sweet."

"She is," I agree, turning my head to kiss her neck. I feel her shiver. "You're sweeter." I lick her neck lightly, and she laughs. "I want you to meet my parents and have dinner with us. They will be here Friday when Maddi gets off school. Then they'll take her back to Connecticut Saturday."

"I don't know if I can. Lorie is supposed to be coming into town. I told her I'd have dinner with her."

"You can invite her," I say, but her body gets tight.

"Lorie is Tom's mom . . . I don't think that would be wise."

"Is Tom going to be in town, too?" I try to keep the annoyance out of my voice, but it's hard to do.

"No, just her. I . . . Maybe I can see if we can have lunch instead of dinner."

"I'd like that," I agree. She relaxes back against me, and I kiss along her neck.

"I don't really want to see her." Her quiet words give me pause.

"Pardon?"

"Lorie. I don't want to see her. I mean, I *do* want to see her, but at the same time I don't. It's different now. I don't want to hurt her, but I feel like there is no way not to."

"What do you mean?"

"She's the only mother figure that I have ever known, but she's Tom's mom, and we're not together anymore. I love her, but I don't want to talk about Tom. It's inevitable he'll come up, because he's her son."

"I get that."

"She loves him," she says, turning to face me. "I know she's worried about him and what he's going through. I used to be the person that she always shared those worries with, but I'm just not that person anymore. The last time we spoke she started to tell me about what Tom is doing now, but I told her I didn't want to hear about him. She hung up without saying goodbye. She wasn't rude or mean, but I know she was upset."

"It's going to take you both time to figure out how to navigate your new relationship."

"I don't know if we *can* have a relationship anymore, and that hurts, because I love her."

"Just give it time. Be honest with her. If you're uncomfortable and she's not understanding of that, then you'll have to reevaluate things. Until then, just be patient."

"You're pretty awesome, Lucas Fremont." She smiles up at me.

"You are, too." I gather her closer and start to kiss her.

"Courtney, I'm ready for bed!" Maddi yells before I can hit my target.

I smile.

"Coming, sweetheart," Courtney shouts back while turning to look over her shoulder at Maddi, who grins before disappearing into her bedroom. Courtney's eyes return to me. "I love her."

"She loves you, too," I tell her, and her expression softens. "Go on, read to her." I start to let her go, but before I can she wraps her arms around my neck and tugs me down for a kiss.

When she pulls away, her eyes search mine for a long moment before she shakes her head and lets go. I finish washing the last few dishes, then go over to my drawing table and start to work again. When Courtney comes out of Maddi's room a half hour later, she looks exhausted. I want to demand that she spends the night, but instead I order her a cab and make her promise to call when she's home. I walk her downstairs and leave her at the door with a kiss, hating that I won't see her again until tomorrow night.

Chapter 12

Family

Courtney

The cool air brushes against my skin, helping ease some of the tension I realize I'm feeling as soon as I reach the restaurant where I'm meeting Lorie for lunch. I hate being late, but Abby had an emergency meeting with a client and needed me. I sent Lorie a text to let her know I was running twenty minutes behind schedule, but she never replied. I know she was put out by my changing plans from dinner to lunch, but I had to choose between disappointing Lucas or her—and I don't want to disappoint Lucas.

I spot Lorie at a four-top table in the back of the room, and I give the hostess a silent wave to let her know that I'm meeting someone.

"Hi. I'm so sorry I'm late."

As always, Lorie looks sophisticated and elegant. She's wearing a pale-blue, tailored women's pantsuit with a cream silk blouse and pearls around her neck. Her almost-white hair is a little longer than I have ever seen her wear it, but it looks good on her.

"It's not a problem. I got your message." She stands and gives me a hug—one that's warm and tight. More of the tension I was feeling is released as she pulls away slightly to look at me. "You look beautiful. I love your hair."

I instantly reach up to touch my head. I never got my hair colored in the past, but Abby insisted I go with her to her salon for a makeover. I got highlights and lowlights, along with a deep conditioning treatment that seemed to make my hair glow and look perfect without my having to do much to tame it.

"Thank you. I love your hair, too." I smile, and she reaches up to touch her hair the same way I touched mine.

"I found a new stylist. She's amazing. I've already ordered us drinks."

I take a seat and set my purse in the empty space next to me.

"I've missed you."

"I miss you, too," I respond.

"Tell me about your life here," she urges after the waiter comes to take our orders.

Without thinking, I tell her about Lucas and Maddi and work and the house. I see the pain in her eyes as I speak, but I also see understanding.

"You love his daughter," she says. I nod. "Are you in love with him? Lucas, I mean?"

I hate that my happiness might hurt her, but I won't lie.

"I'm falling in love with him. Or maybe I'm already in love with him." I pause. "Things between us are new, and we still have a lot to learn about each other, but he makes me happy."

She takes my hand. "I wish things were different, that . . ." She looks away for a moment. "Don't ever think that I don't want you to be happy, Courtney. I love you like my own flesh and blood. I hate what happened to you. I hate that it was Tom who hurt you—and in turn hurt himself. I wish I could change things for the two of you."

"No one can change things."

"I know," she agrees.

She stays quiet as lunch is brought out. When the waiter leaves, she studies me. I can tell she's worried.

"What is it?" I ask.

She presses her lips together for a moment, then lowers her head.

"You're going to be upset, but I love you. Rememb—"

Before she can finish, a shadow looms over the table. An unwelcome feeling slides down my spine. I look up. When my eyes meet Tom's, I feel betrayed.

"Courtney." He pulls out the chair next to mine, not removing my purse but instead sitting down in front of it.

I look at Lorie, and her eyes fill with tears. I can see she's sorry for putting me in this situation, but that is not going to change what she's already done.

"Give me my purse," I say quietly as I pull my eyes from Lorie to look at Tom.

"I just want to talk."

"And what about what *I* want?" I hiss.

The chatter from people at the tables around us quiets down. I can feel them all turn to watch us.

"I'm only here to apologize." He leans in, and I lean back.

"Please hand me my purse."

"Just hear me out."

My body tightens. I feel trapped. I know he's not going to give me my bag until I hear whatever it is he has to say. "Fine."

He starts to reach out his hand toward me, but my eyes drop to it and narrow. He pulls it back and rests it on his lap. "I'm sorry."

"Thank you. Now please hand me my purse."

"I'm going for full custody of Candice—"

"Good for you." I cut him off.

His jaw tightens. "We always wanted a baby. We always wanted to be parents."

My heart twists as what he's suggesting registers.

"I want you back."

My body goes rigid.

He must be crazy. Does he really think I'm so desperate to be a mom that I'd take him back?

"I've always loved you. If you give me a second chance, we can make this work. We can have the family we always wanted."

"Are you nuts?" My question is whispered, betraying the rage I'm feeling.

"We were happy."

"You are . . . You are . . . You're nuts. Completely off your rocker."

"Courtney."

I don't let him say more. I stand, tossing my napkin on top of my uneaten lunch. "I don't want anything to do with you. And now"—I turn to look at Lorie—"I don't want anything to do with you, either." I look back at Tom, staring him in the eye. "You didn't just hurt me when you had an affair, you killed the love I had for you. You made me see the kind of man you really are."

"Court—"

I hold up my hand. "I hope that one day you find someone to love, Tom. I really do. But that someone is *not* me." I pull in a breath, then hold out my shaking hand. "Please hand me my purse. Do not ever contact me again, or I will be getting a restraining order against you."

"Honey, hand her her bag," Lorie says quietly.

Despite the sadness in her voice, I don't look at her. I'm done.

"Don't be mad at Mom. I made her tell me when you were meeting."

I don't acknowledge his words, I just keep my hand out and my face blank. I want to get out of here. I *need* to get out of here.

With a deep sigh, he reaches behind his back and grabs my purse, then hands it to me. I lift my chin and, without a backward glance, I leave.

I get into a cab right outside. As soon as I'm seated, I call Lucas.

"Hey, baby. How was lunch?" At the sound of his voice, the tears and anger I was holding in are released. I start to cry, not answering his question. "Where are you?"

"In . . . in a ca-cab," I sob into the phone.

"Tell the driver to bring you to my office," he demands.

"I think I should . . . should just go . . . go home."

"Tell the driver to bring you to my office. I'll meet you downstairs."

I don't say okay, I just give the driver the new address. During the ten-minute ride I don't talk to Lucas, but I know he's still on the phone. When I reach his office building, he's standing outside with a worried look on his handsome face. He opens my door and helps me out of the cab before leaning in to pay my fare.

"Come on."

I curl myself under his arm and let him lead me inside the building and up to his floor. Once we are there, the secretary who gave me her shoes the last time I was there starts to smile, but then worry etches her beautiful features. Lucas takes me down the hall into his office and leads me to his couch. He holds me on his lap, murmuring soft words as I cry ugly tears. I tell him about lunch through my sobs. He doesn't say anything, but I feel his tense body coil tighter with every single word.

Eventually my tears dry up. My eyes and body are beyond tired. "I'm sorry," I say, pulling back from his chest to look up at him. "I'm sure you have things to do today."

"Nothing is more important to me right now than knowing you're okay." He rubs his thumbs under my eyes, swiping at the wetness that has coated my cheeks. "I should have known something like this would happen. I should have known he wasn't going to give up."

"I never would have guessed something like this could happen." I drop my eyes.

"Are you crying because of him?"

"No, because of Lorie," I whisper, feeling a fresh wave of tears. "Things . . . I thought things between us . . . It doesn't matter now. I guess I'm crying because now my relationship with her is over, too."

"It doesn't have to be," he says softly.

I shake my head. "It does. I can't trust her. I won't be able to trust her ever again."

"I'm sorry, baby."

"Me too." I cuddle closer to his chest and rest my forehead in the crook of his neck. We sit like that for a long time—until he gets a call that he has to take. Then I lie down on his couch and eventually fall asleep.

When I wake up, he tells me it's time for us to go. We stop at my place, since his parents are picking up Maddi from school. I shower, reapply my makeup, and change. Then we head to his apartment to meet his parents. After what happened today, I'm no longer nervous about meeting his mom and dad. I'm just bone-deep tired.

When we get to his place, he opens the door. I enter before him.

"Courtney!" Maddi shouts, running to me from across the room. I hold out my arms to her, and she buries her face in my stomach for a moment, then looks up at me, grinning. "Linkin talked to me today." Seeing the smile on her adorable face, I smile back, forgetting about everything that happened this afternoon for a moment.

"Did he?"

"Yes! And he sat with me at lunch. He even gave me one of his cookies."

"I think that means he likes you."

"Fuck me," Lucas grumbles under his breath, but I ignore his comment and stay focused on Maddi.

"Did you take it when he gave it to you?"

"It was flaxel seed." Her face scrunches up. "I took it, but I didn't eat it because I don't know what flaxel seed is."

I laugh at her interpretation of *flaxseed*, then wonder what a flaxseed cookie might taste like. Probably not very good.

"We will have to make some chocolate-chip cookies next week. You can take him one," I tell her.

She looks up at me, her eyes shining bright.

God, I love her.

"Well, honey? Are you going to introduce us?" I look away from Maddi and see an older woman and gentleman standing in the middle of the living room. The woman has a bright, welcoming smile on her face that matches her motherly appearance. Her hair just reaches her shoulders and is curled under, framing her face. Her T-shirt is covered in rhinestone flowers of different colors, and her jeans are snug and boot cut over a pair of simple flats. The man next to her is also in jeans, but he has on a green polo shirt that is stretched across his wide chest and stomach. It gives me the impression that he enjoys food and beer. Even at his age, though, he's handsome. I can see that Lucas favors him.

"Mom, Dad, I'd like you to meet Courtney. Baby, these are my parents, Lisa and David."

"It's so nice to meet you both." I start to stick out my hand, but his mom startles me by wrapping her arms around me in a hug.

"It's nice to meet you, too. Madeline hasn't stopped talking about you since we picked her up from school," she says, letting me go.

I look at Maddi, who's standing at my side.

I'm tugged into a hard chest next, then picked up off the ground by David. "Hi, darlin'."

I laugh as he sets me on my feet, then grin as Lucas wraps his arm around my shoulder. "Maddi, honey? Why don't you go change? Once you're done we'll head out for dinner," Lucas says.

I notice that Maddi has her school uniform on—a dark-green polo with the school's emblem on the right breast pocket, khaki pants, and simple white sneakers.

"Okay." She skips off, and I laugh as I watch her go.

"Maddi said Eva's been around a few times over the last week," Lisa says.

Lucas's arm tightens around me. "She has. She moved in with Heather."

"Let me guess . . . The guy she was with got tired of dealing with her bullshit and kicked her out?" David mutters.

"That's my guess, but I haven't asked her about it. All I care about is Maddi's well-being."

Lisa's eyes go to Maddi's closed bedroom door. "She seems happy."

"She *is* happy. I plan on making sure she stays that way," Lucas replies. "I don't want her worried about Eva, so while she's with you this weekend don't talk about her unless she brings her up."

"We don't ever talk about her. She's like Voldemort, She Who Must Not Be Named."

I laugh, and Lisa smiles at me.

"I'm ready." Maddi comes flying out of her bedroom, then skids to a stop. "Where is Merida?"

"She's at home, sweetheart. We can go pick her up after dinner if your dad says it's okay."

She looks at Lucas, who nods, which makes her smile even bigger.

"Wait until you meet Merida, Grandma! She's so cute."

"So ugly she's cute," Lucas says under his breath, but I still hear it and elbow him in the ribs. "What?"

"She *is* cute," I chide.

He smiles. "Whatever."

So she's ugly, but she's loving and cuddly and the perfect dog, as far as I'm concerned.

"I'm starving." David breaks into my stare-down with his son. "Let's go eat. Where are we heading?"

"It depends. What is everyone up for?" Lucas asks as he turns us toward the door.

"Not some fancy place with overpriced dishes and too-small portions. Preferably somewhere I can get an American-made beer in a bottle."

I smile at David, loving him a little already.

"We can go to the Wooden Mill," I suggest. "Abby and I have had lunch there a few times. They have really great food and beer."

"Works for me," David agrees.

We head downstairs and catch a cab so that Lucas's parents can keep their parking spot. When we make it to the restaurant, we are seated almost immediately at a curved booth. I sit on the inside, next to Lucas, with Maddi on my right. Lisa sits next to her, and David at the other end. The waiter comes to take our drink orders. I notice that it feels *normal*—nothing like the dinners I used to have with Tom and his parents, where I was always afraid to eat with the wrong fork. After ordering our appetizers and main courses, we settle into simple, lighthearted conversation. Even though I mostly keep quiet, because they spend a lot of time talking about Lucas's siblings and their kids, I never feel out of place. Lucas never lets me feel that way. He keeps an arm wrapped around my shoulders or a hand resting on my thigh. He touches me, giving me the connection I need. He tells me he likes where I am, likes me at his side. He wants me to know it.

"So, Courtney, what about you—do you have any brothers or sisters?" Lisa asks during a lull in conversation.

I feel Lucas tense next to me.

"I don't—or anyway, none that I know of."

Her eyes fill with confusion when they meet mine.

"I grew up in the foster care system," I explain.

"Oh." She looks briefly at Lucas. "I'm sorry. I had no idea."

"It's okay," I assure her. "I did meet some really great people along the way, but I don't have a family."

"You have us," Maddi says.

My heart seems to stop. I look down at her, and she reaches up, taking my hand.

"We're your family. Right, Daddy?"

Oh my god.

My throat closes up, making it hard to breathe.

"Yeah, honey," Lucas agrees.

I wonder if he means it, or if he's just saying that because he doesn't want to hurt Maddi's feelings—or mine.

"See? You have a family now." Maddi beams at me.

"Thank you, sweetheart." I somehow manage to get that out through the lump in my throat.

"Excuse me," Lisa says, pushing at David to force him out of the booth. She walks quickly away in the direction of the bathroom, keeping her head bowed.

"I'll be back," David mutters as he heads after his wife.

"What happened?" Maddi asks, sounding concerned. She keeps her eyes on her grandparents' backs.

"Nothing, honey." Lucas reaches his arm past me to touch the top of Maddi's head.

I want to get up, but I keep my seat and hold Maddi's hand. When Lisa and David come back to the table, I can see that Lisa has been crying.

"Is everything okay, Grandma?" Maddi asks, not missing anything.

"Yes, honey. You're just so sweet sometimes that Grandma can't handle it." She hugs Maddi, kissing the top of her head. Her eyes meet mine, and she smiles and then reaches over the top of Maddi's hand to clasp mine briefly before letting go.

Thankfully, dinner arrives, and conversation turns back to easy chatter. Through the rest of the meal, my heart feels strange inside my chest—as if it's suddenly too big for the small space.

Chapter 13

AGAIN

COURTNEY

"I cannot fricking believe him," Abby growls into my ear through the phone. "What the hell is wrong with him?"

"It doesn't matter. It's done. I'm done," I say quietly so I don't wake Maddi. She's lying with her head in my lap on the couch.

After dinner, we stopped by my apartment and picked up Merida—along with an overnight bag for me. Lucas insisted I stay with them tonight, and wouldn't take no for an answer. He said he didn't trust Tom not to show up at my place while I was there alone. I tried to tell him that wouldn't happen, but he would not listen. We argued for a good ten minutes before Maddi cut in and said she was ready to go home, so I gave in.

When we got back to Lucas's place, his parents were already there. They stayed long enough to meet Merida and tell Maddi that they would see her in the morning. Once they hugged us all goodbye, Lucas, Maddi, and I settled on the couch to watch a movie. Maddi didn't last long. She fell asleep about twenty minutes ago. When my phone started to ring, Lucas gave it to me and told me it was Abby. I'd already guessed who it was—I had been waiting for her to get back to me since I'd messaged to tell her about lunch.

"I really think I should send his attorney a letter letting him know that his client's continual harassment of you is unacceptable."

"Okay," I agree. The phone goes quiet. "Hello?"

"Okay. So you're going to let me send his attorney a letter?"

"If you think it will help him to see that I'm serious about leaving me alone, yes."

"I do think it will help. Even if it doesn't, at least we will have proof that you've made your feelings known. That way, if he tries to contact you again, we have a reason to move forward with a restraining order."

"Thank you."

"You already know you're welcome, babe. Now tell me how dinner went with Lucas's parents."

"It went really great. They're nice. Normal. Totally the opposite of Tom's mom and dad, which was refreshing."

"I'm glad to hear that." I hear her moving around. "Are you still spending the weekend with Lucas?"

I smile. I can't help it. "Yeah."

"I want all the details Monday—and you'd better not even *think* about holding out on me."

"You know that's not going to happen."

"Don't make me get you drunk," she says.

I laugh. I do have loose lips when I'm drinking, and I would probably tell her every single detail if I were drunk enough.

"Have a good weekend, Abby. Go out on a date. Or at least do something fun."

"I plan on it. Love you."

"Love you, too." I hang up the phone.

Lucas slides my cell from my fingers, then places it back on the coffee table. "What was that about?"

"Abby is going to write a formal letter to Tom's attorney letting him know that his client needs to stop contacting me, and that if he doesn't, we'll pursue a restraining order."

"Good." Lucas looks at Maddi. "I'm gonna put her to bed. Why don't you go get ready yourself?"

My stomach fills with butterflies. The last time I stayed here, it wasn't something I planned. I spent the night sleeping in my clothes. Tonight is different. *We're* different. Things between us are more intense now. I don't know how I will be able to handle sleeping in the same bed as him and not taking advantage. I just can't since Maddi is in the house.

"Sure." I watch him stand. "I should take Merida out," I whisper as he scoops Maddi into his arms.

"I'll take her. Just get ready for bed," he whispers back before carrying Maddi to her room. Merida follows at his heels.

I get up off the couch and head for his room, where he dropped my overnight bag. I grab it and take it with me to the bathroom, then change out of my clothes and into a pair of cotton sleep pants and a matching cotton tank. I tie my hair up into a ponytail and take off my makeup. My stomach is still in knots at the idea of sleeping in a bed with Lucas again. I look at myself in the mirror and frown. I'm not ugly, but I'm also not beautiful like Eva—or skinny like she is, either. When I met her, I felt like I had crawled out from under the rock she used as a throne. I had guessed she was beautiful because Maddi is beautiful, but I didn't know just how gorgeous she was. Her face is model perfect, and I look like the girl next door's stepsister. Her body is toned, and mine is soft. We're complete opposites. Keeping my eyes on my reflection, I suck in my slightly round stomach and stand a little taller, pulling my shoulders back. It changes nothing—I look the same, only uncomfortable.

Putting my extra weight out of my head—since I can't exactly lose twenty pounds before bed anyway—I brush my teeth, apply night cream, and leave the bathroom. When I enter the bedroom, I hear Lucas back come through the front door and then tell Merida to go to Maddi. Unsure what to do with myself, I'm still standing next to the bed when he comes into the room. His eyes sweep over me, then soften before he moves past me to the lamp on the side table. He flips it on, then moves back to the door to shut off the overhead light.

After brushing his lips over my forehead, he whispers, "Get in, baby. I'll be just a few minutes."

I pull back the blankets and slide into bed. I hear the shower start and shiver from the image that pops into my head. I close my eyes and think about puppies and kittens—anything to get my mind off Lucas naked in the shower and the water running over his body. I must do a good job of distracting myself, because I fall asleep.

I slowly wake up, feeling warm and safe. My body is half on top of Lucas. My head is on his shoulder, and his arm curves around me to rest on my hip. My torso is pressed to his, and my thigh is between his legs. I've always loved to cuddle. Tom never did. He would for a while after sex, but eventually he would force me away so that he could sleep. This is only the second time I've spent the night with Lucas, but both times I've woken with him holding me. I open my eyes and notice that the room is barely lit; a small ray of light is coming in through the closed blinds. We agreed to meet Lisa and David for breakfast, with Fawn and Levi, this morning at eight. I don't know what time it is, but I need to shower and get ready, then take Merida out. Plus I don't really feel comfortable with Maddi finding me in her dad's bed—even if she does know I slept here last night.

I start to move away from Lucas, but before I can get anywhere he rolls over, forcing me to my back. His big, warm body comes to rest partly on top of mine, with his knee between my legs. His face goes to the space between my neck and shoulder, and his lips brush against my sensitive skin.

"Good morning," he whispers in a deep voice.

I shiver and slide my hands up his sides, under his arms. "Morning." My voice comes out sultry as his fingers wrap around my side and his thumb brushes across my nipple.

He looks down at me, his face still soft with sleep, his hair mussed. He is always handsome, but looking up at him with my hands on his bare skin, his knee pressed to my core, his weight on me, I've never been more attracted to him.

"You fell asleep on me last night." He moves his thumb across my nipple again, making me squirm.

"Sorry," I breathe.

He grins. "It's all right. I know now you'll be well rested for later on today." He kisses me, pulling my bottom lip between his. I feel his hardness pressed against my side, and I lift my leg, wrapping it around his hip and bringing him closer. I gasp into his mouth when he nudges my core with his knee and at the same time gives another thumb slide across my nipple.

"Lucas . . ." My nails dig into his back. I want him to touch me. My body is throbbing, begging for it. Like he's reading my mind, his fingers slip under the waistband of my sleep pants. He zeroes in on my clit with amazing accuracy, and my hips lift off the bed at the first touch.

His chest rumbles as he groans, "So damn wet." He slides two fingers inside me, making me moan. "I can't wait to feel all of you around me. I can't fucking wait to feel you as you come." His dirty words heat me from the inside out while his thumb circles my clit and his fingers send me spiraling toward the edge. "I want my mouth on you, Courtney. For the next few days, you'll be my breakfast and my dessert."

He speeds up the thrusting of his fingers, and I tuck my head against his shoulder and bite down to keep from screaming out his name as I come. My mind is obliterated, just like the last time he gave me an orgasm. I'm launched into space among the stars. I try to suck in oxygen, but it's almost impossible because his fingers are still gently working me over, causing me to tremble and gasp. I eventually go limp, my legs fall to the sides, and my head falls back to the pillow. When my eyes meet his, he's smiling.

"What?" I ask as I take a deep breath.

"You bit me." He looks down at his shoulder.

I follow his eyes with my own, feeling them widen. Not only did I bite him, I did it hard enough to leave an imprint of all my teeth in his flesh. Around the front edge, it's a deep purple.

"Oh my god. I . . . I'm so sorry. I can't believe I did that to you." I touch the teeth marks softly with the tips of my fingers.

"Baby, this is like a badge of honor." My eyes fly to his. "Knowing I made you come so hard with just my fingers"—he shakes his head—"I can't wait to see how you react when you finally get my cock."

"You did *not* just say that."

"Why not? It's the truth. Have you ever come that hard before?"

"Yes." I leave out that the last time he made me come with his fingers I came just as hard—maybe even harder—only then I wasn't worried about Maddi hearing me, so I didn't bite him.

"Yeah, with me," he says smugly.

I narrow my eyes, wondering if he really can read my mind.

"I need to shower." I pull my hips back, but his fingers don't leave me. Instead he presses them deeper inside me, making me gasp.

"You can't be pissed that you got an orgasm."

"I'm not. I'm pissed that you're smug about giving me an orgasm."

"I've got you under me. There's a lot to be smug about."

"Are you always this annoying in the morning?" I snap.

He grins. "I don't know, but I guess you'll find out."

"Maybe I won't. Maybe you'll be waking up alone from now on," I say.

He buries his face in my neck and laughs. I want to think he's annoying, but really I love the sound of his laughter—and I really love the way it feels against my skin.

Drawn Into Love

"I won't be waking up alone. If I have my way, I won't be waking up alone ever again." He kisses my neck, then rolls us over.

I blink, realizing we are both somehow now standing next to the bed.

"Go shower." He kisses my nose, then taps my bottom before walking out of the room without a shirt. I watch his muscular back and smile to myself before heading into the bathroom.

~

"Have so much fun! Send lots of pictures to your dad's cell so that I can see them," I tell Maddi, whose arms are wrapped around my waist.

She looks up at me, smiling. "I will." She gives her dad another hug, then heads to the door.

Lisa and David are waiting for her in the hall, talking to Levi and Fawn—whom we had breakfast with this morning. Once she's there, David lifts her up and asks if she's ready to go. She nods at him.

I feel Lucas close by. I lean into him when his arm wraps around my shoulder. I wrap my arms around his middle and rest my head on his chest.

"Love you, Daddy. Love you, Courtney," Maddi giggles over her shoulder at us.

My face softens, and Lucas's hold on me tightens. "Love you, honey," Lucas says, and I hear the smile in his voice.

"Love you, sweetheart," I whisper, not even sure that she hears me as she and her grandparents disappear down the stairs.

"Fawn wants to go to the museum today. You guys wanna come with us?" Levi asks.

"No, we have plans," Lucas says shortly.

I scowl up at him for being rude—even while my whole body seems to go electric.

147

"Figured as much," Levi mutters. "Have a good time." Then his eyes meet mine. "It was nice to finally get to talk to you for more than a few minutes."

"Same," I agree.

I have seen Levi in passing, but never really had the chance to talk to him until today. Just like Lucas, he's easy to talk to, quick to smile, and I really love the way he looks at his wife.

"We will have to have dinner soon," Fawn says, looking between Lucas and me.

"Yeah, but not this weekend . . . ," Lucas mutters.

I roll my eyes while Fawn laughs.

"Have fun." She reaches in, grabbing the door handle and pulling the door closed.

"You too," I say as the door shuts. I look up at Lucas. "Can you not be rude to your brother and Fawn?"

"I wasn't rude," he lies.

I narrow my eyes on his. "Yes, you were."

"No, *rude* would have been me telling him that we couldn't go with them because I plan on spending the day inside of you."

"Seriously?" My face heats, and he grins.

"Seriously." He pulls me so that we are chest to chest, then starts walking me backward—toward his bedroom.

"I just remembered that I have things to do today. I need to do laundry, clean my apartment, and wash my hair," I tell him.

His grin broadens. "You don't."

"I do."

"You don't—especially since there is no reason for you to even *wear* clothes for the next forty-eight hours. And I'll wash your hair, when we take a shower together."

"So your plan is to keep me here as your naked hostage?" I raise a brow.

"That wasn't my plan, but I do like the sound of it now that you say it." He dips his head and nips my neck, then licks over the same spot. "Maybe I should go ask Levi if he has a pair of cuffs I can borrow."

"Oh my god," I breathe as he presses me down so I'm forced to fall back on the bed with him looming over me.

"I like that, too. Feel free to call me god when you come."

"You're so arrogant."

"Mmm."

His eyes roam over me while his hands slide up my T-shirt. His palms skim up my waist, and my breath locks in my throat when he cups both my breasts through my bra. He lowers both cups, then ducks his head and pulls one nipple into his mouth before moving to my other breast and giving it the same treatment.

"Still thinking about the laundry you need to do?" His warm breath brushes across my nipple as he speaks.

"Shut up," I moan, sliding my hands into his hair and holding on as he pulls my nipple back into the warmth of his mouth. I lock my legs around his hips, and he grinds against me. I feel his length even through both our jeans.

He pulls away and growls, "That's not very nice." Then his mouth captures mine, his tongue slips between my parted lips, and I whimper down his throat, clinging to him. He leans back just long enough to pull my shirt up over my head; then one hand slides behind my back and deftly unhooks my bra. He tosses it over his shoulder. I tug at his shirt until he helps me out by taking it off. The feel of his skin against mine makes my whole body heat.

"Help me out, baby. Get out of your jeans," he groans, unfastening his own jeans while I fumble with the button on mine.

I want to scream, "Hallelujah!" once I finally get them unhooked and he begins to tug them down my thighs along with my panties.

As soon as we are both naked, his large palms rest against my inner thighs and he looks down at me.

His fingers run through my folds, through the wetness that he created. The touch makes my hips jerk.

"Lucas . . ." His name comes out raspy, and my fingers curve around his waist.

"This is probably going to go really fucking fast. I promise I'll make it up to you."

I don't have a chance to ask him what he means. I feel the head of his cock slide up and down my slit once, then twice before he fills me in one deep thrust.

"Oh god," I moan, seeing stars.

I have never felt so full, so stretched, so complete in my life.

He goes still. "Look at me, Courtney."

I focus on his handsome face, and I can see the strain in his eyes as he tries to get himself under control.

"Please move." I swivel my hips, and we both moan in unison.

He pulls out slowly, then slides back in, hitting someplace deep inside me that I didn't even know existed until this moment.

I lift my legs and wrap them higher around his waist. I pull his mouth down to mine, grasping his hair with my hands. He groans into my mouth, and my core spasms as his thrusts speed up. Leaning back, he cups one breast and plucks my nipple, sending a shock wave through me.

"I knew you'd feel good, but I still had no idea *how* good," he growls against my mouth as he pounds into me harder.

"I'm close." My legs tighten, and my nails dig into his flesh. "I'm so close."

I match him thrust for thrust, and we both fall over the edge at the same time, breathing into each other's mouths as we connect in the most primal way and lose ourselves in each other. My body feels like dead weight, but I don't let go of him. I bury my face in the crook of his neck as he settles on top of me. His heart pounds against my chest, and mine returns the favor as we try to get our breathing under control.

"You okay?" He pulls back to look down at me, and I nod. "You're crying." He lifts his hand and swipes my cheeks. "Did I hurt you?"

"No." It's not a lie. He *didn't* hurt me, but what he doesn't know is that he now has the ability to without even trying—because I'm not falling in love with him anymore, I *am* in love with him.

"Why are you crying?"

"I don't know." I blink away the tears filling my eyes. When I can see him clearly, I notice that his expression is soft and warm.

"Do you know how much you mean to me?" he asks, gently sliding his fingers down the side of my face.

I shake my head no.

"I—" he starts, but his words are cut off when someone rings the bell. "Ignore it," he says. "Fuck," he growls when it rings again.

"It might be important," I say.

With a reluctant nod, he pulls out of me.

"Do not move," he orders, tossing the sheet over me before getting up and pulling on his jeans, which he leaves unbuttoned. He kisses me swiftly before leaving the room.

I hear him in the living room, then he barks into the intercom. "What?"

"Lucas, is Maddi still here?" I hear Eva's voice whip through the quiet apartment through the intercom.

My eyes widen, and I roll to the side of the bed, taking the sheet with me. I don't hear his reply in my rush to grab my jeans and panties. I tug them on. I put on my bra and T-shirt. I'm running my fingers through my hair when Lucas comes back into the bedroom looking ready to commit murder.

"Is everything okay?"

"We're going to your place," he states.

"What?" I blink at him as he stops in front of me.

"Between your ex and mine, I choose yours. So we're going to your place for the rest of the weekend."

"What?" I repeat.

"Eva *knew* Maddi was leaving with my parents early, and what time they were going. She still came over, and I know it wasn't to tell Maddi to have a fun trip. I know it was to try and fuck up what just happened between me and you."

"Oh." I look over his shoulder at the door, expecting Eva to waltz into the room any second.

"We are not going to stay here, where she can find ways to annoy me. Let's get a shower, then head out."

"Shower . . . ," I breathe.

He smiles a cat-that-got-the-cream smile; then his eyes travel down my body and his smile disappears.

"You got dressed."

"Well, I heard Eva at the door," I explain.

He looks annoyed again. "We'll shower at your place. I'll pack a bag." With that he gives me a hard kiss, then goes to his closet and pulls down a black duffel bag. I watch his shirtless back as he packs before I go and gather up my own stuff.

When it's time to leave, we find Merida asleep on Maddi's bed. She's reluctant to leave her spot, probably thinking that Maddi will be back soon. Eventually, with the promise of treats, I get her off the bed and attach her leash.

We leave the building and, thankful Eva isn't hanging around outside, catch a cab to my place, where we spend the rest of the weekend wrapped up in each other. Unfortunately, Lucas never gives me a chance to wear the bodysuit for him, not that I'm complaining.

Chapter 14

BIRTHDAY PARTIES AND REALITY CHECKS

COURTNEY

"You need to be quiet so you don't wake Maddi," Lucas groans against my neck while sliding his cock inside me from behind and strumming his fingers over my clit. I gasp and then bite down on my bottom lip so I don't moan out loud. When I woke up with him behind me, one hand cupping my breast and the other circling my clit, I was already primed and on the brink of coming.

It's been almost a month since we spent our first weekend together, and since then I've spent every night in Lucas's arms. The day Maddi came home from her grandparents', she asked if I was staying the night. Lucas immediately said yes. I'm not complaining—I love being with my man and my girl. I love waking up under the same roof as them and coming home to them after a day at work.

They are the family I have always searched for, the family I wanted to build for myself. Things feel right. I feel at home, at peace. I often find myself wondering what would have happened if Tom hadn't cheated. Looking back, I realize I wasn't happy, and hadn't been for a long time. I don't think Tom was happy, either. Well, obviously he wasn't, since he was looking elsewhere while married to me. Still, if things didn't happen the way they did with Tom, I wonder if I would have stayed with him. It's hard to think about, because I can't imagine not having this—not having Lucas and Maddi in my life. I love both of them.

"You're being a very good girl. So quiet while you take my cock." Lucas's deep voice makes me shiver. I press my ass back, forcing him deeper. "Such a good girl." He nips my ear.

"Lucas . . ."

"Give me your mouth." I turn my head toward him, and he thrusts his tongue into my mouth, kissing me hard while he pinches my clit. I come in an instant, whimpering into his mouth. He thrusts deep twice more before planting himself to the root inside me. Both of us breathe heavily. "I love waking up to you."

"Do you?" I lean back to see his face, and his eyes search mine.

"Mmm." He kisses me again as he pulls out, then he rolls me to my back. He looks down at me, running his fingers through my hair. "Are you happy?"

"Yes," I whisper, lifting my hand to touch my fingers to his jaw. "Are you?"

"Happy?" he asks. I nod. "Happier than I have ever been in my life."

My face softens. "Do you . . . do you think Maddi is happy?"

"If you have to ask that question, baby, you're not paying attention. I don't think I have ever seen her so happy."

"Really?"

"She's living in a house with two people who love her."

"I do love her," I say, leaving out that I love him, too. I don't want to ruin this by admitting my feelings too soon—even if I do love him.

"I know you do." He places another kiss against my lips. "Now if we could just figure out a way to make Eva step up and be the mom Maddi needs her to be, we'd be golden."

His words make my heart ache. Eva has been around a few times over the last month, mostly showing up out of the blue to pretend like she wants to see Maddi and then hardly sparing her a glance. She's always more focused on trying to get a rise out of Lucas or attempting to intimidate me with catty words and dirty looks.

I hate her. Okay, *hate* is a strong word. I don't hate her, but I don't understand her at all. There are millions of women who would give anything to be a mother, and it seems to me that she just doesn't care at all about the gift she was given. I wish I could make her understand, make her realize how blessed she is to have Maddi as her daughter. But I don't think that will ever happen.

"She's still planning on coming to the party and bringing the stuff you asked her to bring, right?"

I've discovered that Eva has a way of backing out of things and leaving Maddi twisting in the wind. Just last weekend, she was supposed to take Maddi shopping but canceled at the last minute, saying something had come up and she couldn't make it. I ended up taking Maddi to get manis and pedis to get her mind off it, but I knew that she was upset about not being able to spend time with her mom—even if she hid it well. It worries me how good she is at hiding her disappointment. She never says she misses Eva, but I know she must. I don't know my mom, but a part of me has always missed her, or the idea of her.

"She says she's coming." Lucas brings me out of my thoughts, and I focus on his eyes, which are filled with annoyance. "Hopefully she actually shows up to spend time with her daughter—and not just to mess with me."

"Whatever happens, we will make sure Maddi has a good day," I tell him.

His expression shifts, and his eyes fill with a look that looks a lot like . . . love.

"Yeah, we will."

I lean up and touch my mouth to his. "I need to shower. Do you mind taking Merida out?"

"Baby, since you've been staying here, when have you *ever* taken her out in the morning?" I press my lips together, and his eyes drop to my mouth. "Exactly."

"I'd like to remind you that you won't *let* me take her out in the mornings."

"I won't," he agrees. "You take three times as long to get ready as I do."

"I do not."

"You do."

"I don't." I narrow my eyes, getting annoyed.

"Baby, just yesterday it took you a year to sort yourself out before we could leave for dinner."

"It did *not* take me a year."

"Okay, half a year." He grins.

"You're annoying."

"I wasn't complaining," he says, still grinning.

"It sounds to me like you're complaining."

"I fucked you against the wall as soon as we got home from dinner. I couldn't even wait until I had you in bed, I wanted you so badly."

My stomach drops as his face gets closer to mine.

"The hair, makeup, and dress had me hard as a rock throughout dinner. Believe me—I'm not complaining."

"Okay," I breathe.

A new wave of desire rushes over me as I remember exactly how we went at it last night. Instead of going over to pick up Maddi from Fawn's as soon as we got home from our date, Lucas led me right into the apartment. He took me against the wall, right next to the door. It was hot—hotter than anything we've done, and we've done a lot—and all of it has been amazing.

"Now go shower while I take Merida out for her walk."

"Sir, yes sir," I say sassily.

His eyes darken with lust. "As a thank-you, you can call me sir later." He kisses me, hard, then rolls out of bed, pulling me up with him.

I'm wearing his T-shirt, which falls to my knees. He grabs a pair of sweats and then comes back to me and slides his hand up my waist, bunching the shirt as he goes. My breath catches as he pulls it off over my head, leaving me naked.

"Shower," he orders, putting on his shirt.

I roll my eyes but head for the bathroom, start up the shower, and then take a "year" to get ready—because my man likes the way I look when I do.

～

"Courtney!" calls Libby, Fawn's sister, as soon as I come through the front door of Princess Pizza with a life-size unicorn balloon and a mass of smaller pink, purple, gold, and turquoise balloons trailing behind me.

"Hey." I smile, unable to wave because I'm also carrying a large plastic bag filled with other supplies.

Libby leaves the back of the kitchen, steps out around the counter to greet me with a hug, and takes the plastic bag from me.

"You look beautiful. Then again, you always look like you just stepped off the runway," I say, taking in her jeans, tight tank top, and heels.

"Me? Please. I'm in love with your outfit. Where did you get it?"

"I don't remember. I've had it forever." I smile, looking down at myself. I wanted to be casual but cute today, so I settled on my butterfly-sleeve chiffon top that is cream with black polka dots. I tucked it into my Empire-waist black skirt that flares out and ends just above my knees. Then I added a thick brown leather belt with a bow that matches my wedge heels.

"Well, I'm going to see if I can find the same look somewhere. You always look so put together."

"Thanks." I smile at her, then look around. "Has Eva shown up yet?"

"No." She frowns. "Was she supposed to?"

"Yeah. She is supposed to bring drinks, chips, and snacks for the parents."

"Oh." She frowns again. "Hopefully she'll be here soon."

"Hopefully," I agree. "Where do I need to put these?" I gesture up to the balloons I'm still holding.

"Oh, right." She laughs, taking my elbow and leading me to a room at the back of the pizzeria.

As soon as we walk through the door, my smile gets huge. I know Maddi is going to flip when she sees the decorations that Libby put up. In the middle of the room are three long tables covered in white tablecloths. Against the back wall is a large image of a unicorn with pink sparkly ears, black lashes, and a golden horn adorned with a bouquet of paper flowers like a crown. On the other walls are pink, turquoise, and purple streamers—and more unicorns of different sizes.

"Maddi is going to love this. You did amazing," I tell Libby, meeting her gaze.

"I hope so. I kinda stole the idea for the big unicorn from Etsy." She laughs.

"It's perfect." I walk to the back table, which holds a large white box.

"That's her cake. They delivered it about twenty minutes ago. It's so adorable." She opens the lid for me to get a peek.

"They did a great job."

The cake is the same kind of unicorn that is on the wall, except there is a horn protruding from the cake, along with icing flowers. It's cute—and so Maddi.

"I'm just going to place the balloons around the room. If you want, you can set up the plates and things that you brought with you on the tables." She trades me the bag she's carrying—which has plates, cups, and utensils in it—for the balloons. "Antonio is going to bring another table in for gifts so they'll be out of the way."

"Sounds good," I say.

She starts placing balloons around the room while I set up the tables with the plates, table decorations, and gift bags Maddi and I made up a few nights ago. Each bag contains bubbles, a candy ring, glitter lotion, plastic bangles, and a few pieces of chocolate.

I glance at my watch when we are done and realize that Maddi and Lucas should be here any minute. Lucas and I agreed that I would come early, since we wanted the balloons to be a surprise for Maddi.

"I'm going to go back to the kitchen to finish getting stuff ready," Libby says. "When Maddi and the kids get here, we will start bringing out the stuff for the pizzas."

"Let me know if you need any help," I say.

She waves my offer away. "No help needed. The rest is easy. The kids will do most of the work. Let me know if you need anything."

"I will."

She smiles at me once more before leaving.

I look at my watch again and try not to get annoyed with Eva, who's still not here. If she flakes, we won't have drinks for the kids or snacks for the parents.

"Baby," Lucas calls from the doorway.

I turn to find him looking as handsome as ever in a pair of dark jeans, a black T-shirt that fits his frame snugly, and boots. Maddi is wearing the colorful tutu Fawn got for her—over bright-pink leggings—and a T-shirt that says "Birthday Girl" in glitter. A sleep mask that looks like a unicorn's face is covering her eyes.

I walk toward Lucas and Maddi. I lean up to kiss his cheek, then bend down to whisper in Maddi's ear, "Are you ready, sweetheart?"

"Yes." She smiles so bright that I don't have to see her eyes to know they are filled with excitement.

"All right." I step to her side and rest my hand on her shoulder.

Lucas takes off her blindfold, saying, "Happy birthday, honey."

I watch her take in the room, the decorations, and the cake that is now unboxed. I fight the urge to cry when she turns back toward us and throws her arms around our waists.

"I love you guys."

"Love you, too, sweetheart." I rest my hand on the top of her head, then look at Lucas when I feel his eyes on me. He doesn't say anything— then again, he doesn't have to. I see in his eyes that he's happy because his baby is happy.

"Go check out your cake, honey," Lucas says.

Maddi looks up at both of us and smiles before she skip-hops across the room toward her cake.

"Is Eva here?" he asks when she's out of earshot.

I shake my head no.

"The party is going to be starting in just a few minutes," he says angrily.

"I know," I agree. Then I add, "Do you want to call and see if she's on her way? If she's not, I'm going to have to run out to get drinks and stuff."

"Fuck." His jaw clenches as he pulls out his cell phone and walks out of the room, putting it to his ear.

I watch him for just a second before I head across the room toward Maddi. She's now wandering down the length of each table, looking at everything.

"What do you think, sweetheart?"

"It's so cool." She beams at me.

"There is one more thing . . ." I open my purse and pull out the headband I got her. It's covered in multicolored silk flowers and has a gold unicorn horn in the middle. I place it on her head. "Perfect." I reach into my bag and pull out my compact mirror for her to see.

"I love it," she breathes. "Thank you, Courtney. I love you so much."

"You're welcome, sweetheart. I love you so much, too." I rest my hand against her soft cheek and fight back a wave of tears.

"Baby?" Lucas calls from the doorway. He jerks his chin up—a silent signal for me to go to him.

I nod, then focus on Maddi once more. I try to ignore the obvious worry I see in her eyes. She might not know exactly what's going on, but she knows her dad well enough to know he's not happy about something.

"Why don't you take that big unicorn balloon and tie it to wherever you're going to sit?"

"Okay," she agrees. Then she asks, "Is my mom still coming to my birthday?"

Gahhh! Maybe I actually do hate Eva.

"I don't know, sweetheart. But I do know that your friends will be here soon, and we are going to have so much fun today." I put on a smile, and she smiles back, but her smile is just like mine—totally fake. "Go pick your seat," I urge. She nods and heads away from me.

I walk toward Lucas. Even before I get to him, I feel his pissed-off vibe coming my way. "She's gonna be late. She said she's got the drinks and stuff but won't be here for an hour and a half."

"At least she's coming," I tell him quietly.

"Yeah. At least she's coming to her own child's birthday party," he says sarcastically. "Even if she isn't doing it on time or doing something she promised me she would do, which is to bring the drinks and shit for the party." He runs his fingers through his hair.

I get closer to him and rest my hand on his bicep. "It's going to be okay. I can run across the street to get some stuff to hold us until Eva gets here."

"I know you'll do that, baby. It also fucking kills me that you have to do that."

"It's not a big deal."

"It is."

"Okay, it is, but you need to take a breath. Maddi knows something is off right now, and you looking like an angry bear isn't going to make her feel any better."

His eyes go across the room, and his expression shifts. "You're right."

"I know. Now put on a happy face so you don't scare the kids or the other parents," I say quietly.

His eyes come to me and soften. "I"—my heart speeds up—"lo—"

"Madeline!" Three girls shriek in unison as they plow by us and head right for Maddi, cutting off whatever Lucas was going to say.

I laugh as they all hug Maddi. Then I feel Lucas's fingers brush mine. My pointer finger wraps around his, and I lean into him for a second before murmuring, "I'm going to run across the street and get some drinks and chips."

"All right, baby." I feel his lips touch the top of my head, and I smile before I go across the room to get my bag. When I make it back to him, he's holding out a wad of cash for me.

"I have money."

"Yeah." He shoves the money into my hand, ignoring my comment.

I don't argue with him since I know it will be pointless. He never lets me pay when we are out to dinner or at the grocery store. I've given up trying.

"I'll be back," I say as he presses a quick kiss to my lips.

When I make it back to the party about twenty minutes later, there are little girls filling every single seat and parents lining the walls, chatting and laughing. I start to take the drinks and things to the table with the cake, but notice that there are already drinks out, along with bowls filled with chips and platters covered in finger foods.

I look around the room. My eyes meet Eva's. If looks could kill, I'd for sure be dead. I don't know why she lied about being so late—and I really don't care. All I care about is that Maddi has all the people she cares about here. I tuck the bags away under the table, then feel Lucas get close to my back.

"She showed up not even five minutes after you left." His hand wraps around my hip, and his mouth rests next to my ear.

"At least she showed."

"I wish I had your outlook on things," he mutters.

I sigh. "Remember, you're not allowed to scare anyone with your angry-bear vibes."

"I remember." I hear the smile in his voice, and I turn to look up at him over my shoulder. "Thank you, baby," he says.

"For what?"

"For being you."

"I am kind of awesome," I joke.

He shakes his head, his expression turning serious. "You don't realize how amazing you are." My body melts into his. "You don't know how grateful I am that I found you—for not only me, but for Maddi, too."

Tears sting the backs of my eyes, and I turn toward him and rest my hands against his chest. "Don't make me cry in a room full of total strangers—and your ex-wife."

"All right, I won't make you cry." He cups my cheek and slides his fingers along my jaw. "I just need you to know that we both lo—"

"Lucas. Courtney." Eva's friend Heather cuts off Lucas's words.

I want to scream at her to go away. Then I want to find a scientist, a witch, or a warlock to turn back time so I can rewind a few moments and hear what Lucas was going to say to me before she opened her big mouth and ruined the moment.

"Heather," Lucas growls.

I move to his side, then elbow him in the ribs.

"You do know this is a party for kids, right?" he asks her.

My eyes widen when I realize what he means. Heather is dressed for a night out on the town, not a birthday party for seven-year-olds. Then again, Eva is dressed almost the same way. Both of them are wearing skintight dresses, high heels, and way too much makeup.

"I know," she laughs. "Me and Eva have dinner plans after this, so we came dressed for that." She waves off his comment, then looks around the room. "Is Levi going to be here today?"

I wonder why she's asking about Levi.

"No. He's not coming. Even if he were, he'd walk out if he saw you here."

"Why? We used to be friends. I still care about him."

"Then you'll be happy to know he's happy—and his wife is pregnant. They are over-the-moon excited to become parents."

"Oh." She licks her lips. "Good for him."

"Yeah. Good for him," Lucas agrees.

"Well"—she looks around—"Madeline looks happy. It's cool you threw this party for her." With that, she walks off.

I look up at Lucas. "She dated Levi," he says.

"Oh . . . ," is all I can say, even though I can't picture Levi with her, not after seeing him with Fawn. "Is Fawn really pregnant?"

"Yeah, but they aren't telling anyone yet."

A pain I haven't felt in a while fills my chest. It's so odd being happy for someone while feeling totally devastated at the same time. For years I've gotten this feeling anytime someone I knew became pregnant.

"I'm happy for them."

"Me too, baby." He smiles, then his eyes turn questioning. "How many kids do you want?"

My chest gets tight, and my stomach drops at his question. "I . . ."

"I'd like a couple more. Or at least one more—a boy."

Oh god.

A vision of a tiny baby boy who looks like Lucas fills my mind. My chest gets even tighter, and bile crawls up the back of my throat.

"What about you? How many kids do you want?"

"I . . ." I look past him for an escape, feeling the floor under me shaking. Or maybe it's my legs shaking. I don't know.

"Who's ready to make some pizzas?" Libby shouts, pushing a metal cart into the room.

Relief floods through my veins. "I should help her," I say, not looking at Lucas. I *can't* look at him. I don't know why I haven't told him yet that I'm broken. That with me, he could never have more kids. I have been so filled with the family he's given to me in Maddi that I almost forgot.

But how could I forget?

"She's okay, baby. She does this every weekend," Lucas says, wrapping my hand around my hip to keep me hostage.

"Right," I agree quietly.

His lips touch the side of my head. Then, for the rest of the party and the rest of the night, I pretend that everything will be okay.

Even though I know it won't be.

Chapter 15

ALL I NEED

LUCAS

"I think I should go home."

At Courtney's statement, my eyes meet hers. I noticed yesterday as the birthday party carried on that she seemed a little off. I figured she was just annoyed with Eva and the shit she had pulled. When we got home from the party, we didn't talk about it because Maddi had two friends sleeping over. We also didn't talk about it when we went to bed, because two seconds after Courtney's head hit the pillow she was out. We haven't had a chance to talk today since we spent the morning with three girls who couldn't seem to stop talking. This is the first quiet moment we've had alone, and that's because Fawn and Levi took all three girls to see a movie.

"Pardon?" I lean against the counter and study her.

"I . . . Well, I haven't been home in a week. I think I should go home and check on things," she says as she cleans up the dishes in the sink that are left over from the pancake breakfast she made for Maddi and her friends.

"We can swing by your place tomorrow evening before we go to dinner."

"I . . . I think you should have some time alone with Maddi," she states, not looking at me.

What the fuck?

"Why?" I attempt to keep the growl out of my voice, but know I fail when I see her flinch at my question.

"I've been around every day for almost a month. I think it would be good for Maddi to just have time with you," she says, not meeting my eye.

"Have I—or Maddi—given you any indication that we want that?" I ask, getting angry.

She turns away from me.

"I don't want to fight about this."

"Then why are we even talking about it?" I ask.

Her shoulders slump. "Forget I said anything."

Not likely.

"Talk to me, Courtney," I demand.

"Maybe . . . maybe we *are* going too fast." She keeps her eyes averted.

"Too fast?" I repeat, my hands clenching into fists at my sides.

"Yes. Maybe this is all happening too quickly."

"What exactly are you trying to tell me?"

"I think we need some time."

"Are you fucking with me right now? You've been in my life—and in Maddi's life—for a couple of months now. All of a sudden you're telling me that we are moving too fast and that we need some time?"

"There are things you don't know," she whispers.

Dread fills me as her eyes start to get wet.

"So fucking tell me!" I shout, feeling her slipping away from me.

Merida, who was lying next to the door, jumps up and barks.

"I can't do this." She tries to move past me, but I block her exit.

"Talk to me."

"I need to leave."

"Fucking talk to me." Fear makes me roar out my demand.

"I can't have kids! Okay?" she shouts. My whole frame goes rigid. "I will never be able to tell you how many kids I want—because I can't have *any*."

"Baby . . . ," I whisper, taking another step toward her as I watch her face crumple.

"I'm broken." She covers her face with her hands and sobs.

I close the distance between us and gather her in my arms, pulling her against my chest. She doesn't fight me. Her arms circle my waist, and she holds on tight, crying against my chest.

I place my lips against her ear. "You're not broken, Courtney."

"I am. I'm broken. I should have told you sooner. I just . . . I fell in love with Maddi and you and the life we have been building, and I forgot. I forgot that this *isn't* my life, that Maddi *isn't* mine, and that I won't *ever* be able to have a baby. I should have told you." She cries harder, and my chest feels as if it's cracking open.

"You're perfect. So fucking perfect, baby." I slide my hand up into her hair, cupping the back of her head.

"I should have told you," she repeats once more. "I just haven't thought about my infertility because, with Maddi in my life, it hasn't been on my mind."

"Baby . . ." My voice is thick with emotion.

The pain in her eyes is almost unbearable to witness. "I tried. I did everything in my power to get pregnant. Temps, fertility meds, and IVF, but it never happened."

"Wha—" I start.

"The doctors call it 'unexplained infertility.' They don't know why I can't conceive. I just can't." She drops her forehead to my chest, her shoulders shaking with a fresh wave of tears.

I pick her up and carry her to the bedroom. I lie down with her in my arms. I listen to her cry for a long time. It kills me to hear it, but I do it, holding her tight.

With my lips to the top of her head, I close my eyes. Things start clicking into place in my mind. I hope I'm wrong, but I don't think I am. When her tears die down, I place my fingers under her chin and lift her face so I can look into her eyes.

"Please tell me that fuckwad didn't get his secretary pregnant while you were going through treatments," I say. Her eyes fall closed in a silent answer. "That piece of shit. That motherfucking piece of shit," I hiss out.

She shakes her head, then opens her eyes back up to look at me. "In the beginning, when I found out about his affair, I wished my last round of IVF had worked just so I would have someone to love, someone to love me unconditionally. How screwed up is that?"

"It's not screwed up, baby. Not after how you grew up, and especially not after what you lost. You were married to a man who I'm sure you thought you'd spend the rest of your life with. I understand holding on to something that isn't really there."

"I'm glad it didn't happen," she says quietly. "I'm glad Tom and I didn't have a child who would have had to grow up in the mess that was our relationship."

Her words gut me. Maddi is growing up exactly like that, as much as I wish she didn't have to. Even though I try to protect her, I know she still sees and feels more than she should.

"I should have told you before."

Her words bring me out of my thoughts, and I focus on her once more. "I'm sorry, baby. So fucking sorry you had to go through that. But what you just told me changes nothing, Courtney." I wrap my hands around the sides of her neck and keep hold of her gaze when she tries to lower her head. "If things go the way I think they are going to go, you'll have a daughter in Maddi. If we want more kids, you and I will find a way to make that happen for us."

"Lucas . . ."

"You have to know that Maddi and I both love you."

"I . . ."

"I love you." I tell her something I have been trying to tell her for days now. "I love you. Maddi loves you. Like Maddi said, *we* are your family."

She sobs. I smile, then press my mouth to hers and say, "I'm not letting you go. Or giving you space. Or taking time. This is us. This is our future, our family. I'm happy, Maddi is happy, and I hope like fuck that you're happy, too."

"I am," she says quietly.

"Then all the rest can be figured out."

"You're not mad?"

The simple question catches me off guard.

"The only thing I'm pissed about is that you're upset. If I had known your history, I could have saved you the worry you've been feeling since yesterday. I hate that my question about having kids is what brought this on."

"You know I love you, too. Right?" she asks.

I feel my muscles relax even while my hold on her tightens. I needed to hear that. I didn't know how badly I needed to hear it until right now, but I needed those words from her.

"Thank you for that gift, baby," I say. Her face softens. "I promise to do right by you." I cover her mouth with mine and kiss her deep and wet, then pull back and tuck her head under my chin. "Can I ask you something?"

Her head tips back, and her eyes meet mine. "Anything."

"Have you ever tried to find your parents?"

"I got my records when I turned eighteen, but in the end, I was left with more questions than answers. All I know is that I was left at the hospital after my mom gave birth to me." She pulls in a breath and continues, "I was born two months early—and addicted to crack. I don't know much about my mom besides the fact that she was an addict. She didn't sign my birth certificate."

Christ.

The image of her as a baby, in a hospital all alone, just about kills me.

"I wonder if she thought she was doing the right thing by leaving me there. I wonder if she thought that a nice family would adopt me."

"I bet she did."

I *hope* she did, though I know from a friend who adopted a child that not too many people are willing to take a chance on a drug-addicted baby.

"Can we take a nap?" she asks, pulling me from my thoughts.

I nod. She curls her body around mine, and I hold her knowing I'm holding my future in my arms. A future that I'm really fucking looking forward to. A future where she will never have to worry about being unloved again.

～

Three days later, I listen to Courtney laugh as I place a bright-yellow hard hat on her head. "I probably look like a dorky bumblebee," she says.

I grin, then let my eyes roam over her from head to toe. As usual, she looks beautiful. She's wearing a black silk blouse that gives me glimpses of her black lace bra underneath when she moves a certain way, a tight yellow pencil skirt, and black heels that I'm already imagining digging into my back when I take her in my office.

"You're the sexiest bumblebee I've ever seen," I tell her.

She laughs again, hitting my chest lightly with the back of her hand. Since her breakdown a few days ago, things have been good. Better than good. She seems even more open with me and more affectionate with Maddi, which is something that I wouldn't have thought was possible. She might think she'd forgotten about her infertility, but I think it was still there, in her subconscious, holding her back from us.

"Are you ready?" I ask, putting on my own hard hat.

"As ready as I will ever be."

I take her hand and let her into her house. As soon as we walk through the front door and into the living room, I feel her excitement as she looks around. Even with walls still waiting to be put up and the floors still needing to be put down, the place looks perfect. The stone fireplace is exactly as I drew it up—before I ever met Courtney. I can picture her and Maddi reading a book in front of it, or her curled into my side and watching the TV that will hang above the wooden mantel. She lets my hand go and walks to the kitchen. I see her gaze out the window over where the sink will be.

Something heavy and unwanted starts to fill the pit of my stomach. Courtney and I have never talked about money, not once. I know she works for Abby. I know she goes to work every day, Monday through Friday. But I doubt being a paralegal pays enough to afford this place, the construction, and the apartment she's renting.

"What is it?" At her question, I look at her.

"Nothing." I try to shake off the feeling.

"You didn't let me avoid sharing what was on *my* mind the other day. I don't think I should let you, either."

She's right. If we are going to make this work, we need to be honest with each other always.

"How can you afford this?"

I can see that my question has caught her off guard. I notice her back go straight.

"Tom." My jaw gets hard. She takes a step toward me. "I . . . When I divorced him, I went after him in a way that I thought would hurt him most." She ducks her head, seeming embarrassed by her admission. I see her turn to look at the room again, and guilt eats at me when she continues speaking. "This isn't something that I got for myself. I got this because of Tom, because of his betrayal." Her face pales while nausea twists in my stomach. "Can we go?" she whispers, starting toward the door.

I grab hold of her hand, stopping her. "Look at me, baby," I say softly. She shakes her head. I lift up her chin and see tears pooling in her eyes. "You know I'll never be able to give you this. I'll never be able to give you a life where you can afford a house in this area," I tell her honestly. "I make good money. I'm comfortable, but I don't make the kind of money where I will ever be able to afford a house like this."

"I didn't even *want* this." She closes her eyes, and a single tear falls down her cheek. "When I married Tom, all I wanted was a family of my own who would love me unconditionally. I didn't grow up with much. I never wanted to be rich, I just wanted to be loved."

"I can give you that," I say. Her head flies up, her eyes searching mine. "I can give you love and family, in me and Maddi."

"I . . ."

"I'm not wealthy," I state.

"I don't care about money, Lucas." She rests her hands against my chest. "I really don't. I never have. Money didn't dry my tears or ease my pain when Tom stepped out on our marriage. Money didn't hold me at night, make me feel safe, or give me the love of a child who's not my own but who I love like she is. *You* did that."

Fuck, her words kill me.

"I love you," I get out through the tightness in my throat.

"I know." She smiles, leaning deeper into me. "Family is what is important to me. Your love and Maddi's. I would live in a cardboard box on the side of the road as long as you and Maddi were there with me."

"Let's hope that never happens," I mutter.

She smiles, then tips her head to the side, asking, "Would *you*?"

"Would I what?"

"Would you live in a cardboard box with me?"

"Yes." My answer is firm.

"Would you live *here* with me?" She looks around. "I know it's not much to look at right now, but I think that with the right touch we can turn this place into a beautiful home for our family, don't you?"

I know she's trying to joke in order to make me relax. She knows that I'm the kind of man who pays for dinner—and whatever else comes up. She gets that me moving into a home she paid for would be me putting my pride aside.

"I'd live anywhere with you."

"Do you think Maddi will like the house?"

"Baby, you know you don't even have to ask that question. She'd love having an actual room. But more than that, she'd love having a bathroom to herself."

"So is this a plan?" she asks, relaxing against me.

I pull her even closer with my hands on her hips.

"No."

She starts to pull away.

"Before we move in here, I need to put a ring on your finger."

"What?" Her eyes widen.

"You didn't expect to live in sin with me, did you?"

"You want to get married. To me?"

"I sure as fuck don't want to marry anyone else. Don't you want to get married?"

"Yes." Her bottom lip trembles.

"Then that's the plan. We get married, then we move in here."

"I'm going to cry." Her voice shakes.

"You can't cry." I touch my mouth to hers. "You need to be able to see the rest of the house so you can sign the papers, and you won't be able to do that if you're crying."

"Right." She waves her hand in front of her face, holding her eyes open in an attempt to dry them out.

I laugh, then take her hand and lead her through the rest of our house.

After we leave, we head to my office. She signs the papers for the contractor. When she's done, I get my wish to feel her heels in my back.

I fuck her quietly on my office desk before we both have to get back to work.

~

When I see Eva's name pop up on my phone screen, I stop just outside the door to the apartment and set the bag of Chinese food at my feet. Not wanting Maddi or Courtney to hear what I'm about to say, I move to the second landing of the stairs and keep an eye on the door as I put the phone to my ear.

It's been a little over three weeks since Maddi's birthday. That was the last time I heard from Eva. Last weekend she was supposed to take Maddi overnight, and that had been the plan for more than a month. She didn't show, didn't call, didn't answer my calls or return any of my messages when I tried to get ahold of her repeatedly.

I'm done with her bullshit, done setting up Maddi and watching her fall every time Eva lets her down. I talked to my lawyer—along with Abby—and they both agree that since I have full custody of Maddi, I'm within my rights to keep Maddi from Eva until she gets a lawyer. I hate doing this, but I'm at the point where protecting Maddi from further hurt is all that matters.

"Lucas . . . ," Eva says softly as soon as I answer. My teeth grind together. "I . . . Do you have time to meet me for a drink so we can talk?"

Is she fucking crazy?

"No," I grit out. "I'm done, Eva. So fucking done with your bullshit. Unless you get a lawyer and file for some type of visitation with the court, you will no longer have access to Maddi. No more broken promises. No more fucked-up stops at the apartment to spread your bullshit. Nothing. Do you understand that?"

"I'm back with Tyler," she hurries to get out.

Rage fills the pit of my stomach.

I should have fucking known.

"I-I wanted to call to cancel last weekend, but we were out of the country, and I didn't have service."

"She was devastated, Eva," I say, trying to control the fury that is filling my veins. "She was devastated that you didn't show, that you didn't call. That you let her down once a-fucking-gain."

"I'm sorry. I just . . . I had to think about my future. I needed to give Tyler another shot. I needed to focus on him and me."

"Right." I rub the bridge of my nose. She's never going to get it. She will never understand what she's done to Maddi. She's too self-centered to understand. "Good luck with everything. I hope you get what you deserve."

"Will you tell her?" she asks as I start to pull the phone from my ear.

"Tell her what?"

"That . . . that I won't be around much. That I'm moving back in with Tyler?"

"Yeah, I'll tell her. But Eva, I'm dead fucking serious about what I said. I'm not doing this anymore. I'm not going to let you continue to hurt her. You want to see her, get a fucking lawyer."

"I do love her," she says.

I start to open my mouth to say, "Not enough," but she hangs up before I can. I'm sure she cares for Maddi in her own way, but she *doesn't* love her enough. She sure as fuck doesn't love her the way a mother should love her child.

If I didn't have my family and Courtney, I'd be worried about Maddi's future. But thankfully I don't have to worry about that. Maddi will grow up knowing she's loved, and hopefully we can all love her enough to make up for the lack of love from her mother.

After a few deep breaths I head up the steps, pick up the Chinese food, and put the key in the lock. I push open the apartment door.

The sight that greets me lets me know things will work out. Maddi, Courtney, and Merida are right where I left them when I went to pick up dinner—cuddled up on the couch, watching a movie together. When they see me come through the door, both my girls smile. I smile back, knowing everything is going to be okay.

Chapter 16

Four-Hour Secret

Lucas

I settle into one of the wicker chairs on my parents' back deck, beer in hand. My dad and brothers—Levi, Cooper, and Cole—take their own seats. I haven't had much time alone with my dad or my brothers since we arrived yesterday for the Thanksgiving weekend. Courtney insisted we come to my parents' for the holiday so she could spend some time with my parents, my brothers, and their wives.

"So when are you asking Courtney to marry you?" This isn't the first time Levi's asked me that question.

"Soon," I respond, taking a pull from my beer.

Really soon.

Ever since the day I told Courtney I wanted to marry her, I've wanted to ask—but I first had to find the perfect ring. I also need to make sure Maddi's okay with it. In my gut I know she will be, but I want her to know that her opinion is important to me. She's blossomed over the last few months from having two people around her showing unwavering love and support. I don't want to sidetrack that progress.

"I like her," Cole says, looking into the house through the sliding door.

Ruby, his wife, and Allison, Cooper's wife, are cleaning up dinner with Fawn and Courtney. The kids are off in the living room watching TV or tearing shit up with their grandma, who I'm sure is encouraging their bad behavior.

"I do, too. She's nothing like Eva," Cooper says, taking a pull from his own beer.

"She's the best thing that ever happened to me," I admit, looking around the table.

I know they all get it. Each of their wives is a strong woman. A woman who would do anything for her family. A woman who loves her husband beyond reason. I never knew what I was missing until I had that for myself.

"Maddi loves her, too," I state.

"There's a lot to love," Dad says. I focus on him. "You did good. I'm happy for you, and your mom's happy for you."

"Thanks, Dad." I take another pull from my beer to wash away the sudden tightness in my throat.

My parents were worried about me when I told them that I was having a kid and marrying Eva. They didn't agree with me getting married to someone just because we were having a child together, but I didn't listen to their advice when I should have.

"Do you plan on moving back here after you two get married?" Cooper asks.

"No, we're settled in the city. Maddi is happy, Courtney has her job there, and I'm so busy that I have to turn clients away on a weekly basis. I didn't think I would ever love any place more than here, but I'm finding that I enjoy living in New York."

"What about you?" Cooper asks, looking at Levi. "Do you plan on moving back once Fawn has the baby?"

"Nope." He shakes his head.

"Maybe Cole and I should talk the girls into moving to the city. I'm sure they could find a spot to open a bakery."

Ruby and Allison are sisters who own a bakery in town, which is how they met my brothers.

"Your mother would lose her mind if you two left with her grand-babies," Dad says.

Cooper nods, knowing Dad is not lying. My mom didn't take the news that Levi was moving away from our hometown well, but he was single, and she knew that he was going after his dream of being a detective in the city. When I told her that Maddi and I were moving, she cried for two days. She loves having her kids and grandkids close, and if Cooper and Cole told her they were following us to the city, she would probably drive my dad up the wall until he gave in and moved, too.

A loud shriek causes us all to look into the house. Three kids zoom past the sliding glass door, chasing one another.

"I should go check on the kids. Who knows what Mom's letting them get up to?" Cole says.

"I should get Courtney and Maddi back to the hotel." I stand as well, then reach over and pat my dad on the shoulder. "See you in the morning."

"See you then," Dad agrees.

I lift my chin to him and my brothers before following Cole into the house. I stop to give Courtney a kiss—and to let her know that we are going to leave. Then I go in search of Maddi, whom I find in the living room playing with her cousins. When I tell her it's time to head out, she pouts before going to tell everyone goodbye.

"You guys could have stayed here," Mom says.

I smile at her. "I know, but the girls will be more comfortable at the hotel—in an actual bed."

"The pullout *is* a bed." She shakes her head.

"Last time I stayed on the pullout, I couldn't walk right for a week," I remind her. She pouts just as Maddi did moments ago. "We'll be back in the morning to have breakfast before we head back to the city."

"I never see you all anymore."

"You can come see us anytime, too, Mom," I say.

She stands to give me a hug. "I know. I just miss all my boys being under one roof."

"Then maybe you shouldn't have changed out our bedrooms for an office and a sewing room the second we left the house." I grin, and her nose scrunches up. "I'll see you tomorrow."

I kiss her cheek, then go get Maddi and Courtney. We load up the car we rented for the weekend and head to our hotel. Once there, I tuck an already-sleeping Maddi into her bed, then get into bed with Courtney.

"I love your family," she tells me in the dark.

I smile against the back of her head. "They love you, too."

"Can we come back for Christmas?" she asks.

My smile broadens. "Mom would like that."

"Good."

She goes quiet, and I listen to her breathing even out before I follow her off to sleep.

~

"Hey, Daddy." Maddi smiles at me as I walk into her room.

"Hey, honey." I touch the top of her head before taking a seat on the side of her bed.

It's been three weeks since Thanksgiving, and today I picked up Courtney's engagement ring. Now it's time to talk to my baby and make sure she's okay. I watch her play with her dolls on the floor and smile as she lines them all up. I don't doubt she owns all the L.O.L. dolls now—Courtney can't seem to help herself. I think she comes home with one of those plastic balls at least once a week.

"Come sit up here with me, honey. I have something I want to talk to you about." I pat the bed next to me.

She nods, then sets the toy she's holding aside and gets up. She takes a seat next to me, and I turn to face her, taking her hand in mine. I feel nervous even though I know I have nothing to be nervous about.

"Am I in trouble?" She frowns.

"Did you do something that you *should* be in trouble for?" I raise a brow, and she seems to ponder that question before shaking her head no.

"No, you're not in trouble. I want to ask you how you're feeling."

"I'm not sick." Her eyes widen with worry, probably because she has a sleepover planned for the coming weekend.

"I . . ." I smile, then clear my throat. "I mean how do you feel about Courtney and me?"

"Oh. I love Courtney and you."

"What would you think if I said I was going to ask Courtney to marry me?"

"Really?" She smiles. "Are you going to? Is Courtney going to be my mom?"

"Well, she would be your stepmom. But yes."

"Do you think she will let me call her Mom? Do you think I can be the flower girl at the wedding? Can we get a puppy?"

I laugh. I can't help it. "You will have to ask her about calling her Mom, but I bet you she would love it. I'm sure you could be the flower girl. But no, we're not getting a puppy. We already have Merida."

"But Merida needs a friend." She pouts.

She's been saying for weeks that Merida needs a friend because she's lonely when we are all gone during the day. I'm not a dog, but I doubt she's lonely. She's probably happy to have some time to herself when she's not being carted around or dressed up by Maddi, who plays with Merida like she's a doll.

"Sorry, honey. The answer is still no."

"Okay." She sighs.

"So are you okay with me asking Courtney to marry me?"

"Yes! When are you going to do it? Can I help?"

"I'd like that."

"Yay." She hugs me, and I hug her back, holding her tight and soaking in the feeling. "I love you, Daddy."

"I love you, too, honey. Always to the moon and back."

"To the moon and back." She smiles at me, then looks at the bedroom door when she hears Courtney shout that she's home.

Seeing her excitement, I place my finger to my lips. "This has to be a secret for just a few more days. We will ask her this weekend, when everyone is in town for your concert."

"Okay." She nods happily. "I can keep a secret."

"Good." I kiss her forehead, then let her go and watch as she skips out of the room to greet Courtney.

I make it across the apartment to the kitchen before Courtney pulls her eyes from Maddi to look at me and smile. "Hey."

"Hey, baby. How was work?" I kiss her when she tips her head back.

"Work." She shrugs. "What are we doing for dinner tonight?"

"Spaghetti," Maddi says, picking up Merida and hugging her to her chest. "I wanted pizza, but Daddy said that we can't have pizza two days in a row."

"Your dad's right, honey." Courtney grins, then asks, "Did you finish your homework?"

"Not yet." Maddi looks away.

She hates homework. Then again, I don't know many kids who enjoy it.

"All right, I'm going to change. Then I'll help you with your school-work while we cook."

"I got dinner."

"Are you sure?"

"I'm sure." I kiss her again, then watch her and Maddi leave the kitchen and head toward the bedroom.

Maddi talks a mile a minute about school, a swim team at the YMCA that she wants to join, and the boy she likes in her class. As usual, I ignore the last part.

I make dinner while the girls sit at the bar doing Maddi's home-work. When dinner is ready, we eat on the couch and watch TV. It's not long after that I send Maddi to take a shower—and make out with Courtney on the couch.

When Maddi comes back out in her pj's, we watch one of her shows. Then we follow her into her room to read a story and tuck her in.

That's when I learn that Maddi can only keep a secret for approxi-mately four hours.

Sitting on the couch and going over some paperwork from the office, I half listen to the girls in the bedroom.

I hear Courtney ask, "Do you have ants in your pants?"

"No," Maddi giggles.

I wonder what that's about but don't get up to check on them.

"Are you sure?"

"Yes." Maddi laughs again, then blurts, "We're getting married!"

"What?" Courtney laughs.

I get up off the couch and move closer to the door.

"I forgot—it's a secret," Maddi says quietly.

"A secret . . . ?" Courtney sounds confused.

"It's a secret that Daddy is asking you to marry us," Maddi says. "Don't tell Daddy I told you. It's supposed to be a secret."

I listen to Courtney laugh and then say quietly, "I won't tell him. But how do you feel about all of us becoming a family?"

"We're already a family," Maddi responds immediately.

God, I love my baby.

"You're right. We are," Courtney agrees.

She says something after that, but I can't make out what it is because she's talking so quietly. I go back to the couch and get back to work.

When Courtney comes out of the bedroom, it looks like she's been crying. I don't ask why. That moment between the two of them is theirs.

"Maddi wants another dog," she tells me, taking a seat next to me on the couch.

I fight back a smile.

"I think I'm going to get her one when we move."

"Baby, that's not happening," I state.

She turns to face me. "Why not? She's right. Merida does need a friend."

"Merida *doesn't* need a friend." I laugh.

"Well, I think she does."

"Not happening."

"Okay, no dog. What about a cat?"

"No."

"No. No dog, or no cat?" she asks.

"Neither."

"A hamster, then?" she asks hopefully.

I wonder what the hell Maddi said to her. We've been on the same page for weeks about not getting another dog.

"No."

"A rabbit?"

"No."

"A ferret?" she pleads.

"Hell no."

"What you don't know won't hurt you," she mumbles under her breath.

I smile, then tackle her to the couch and loom over her.

"You get another animal, I'll find out."

"Whatever." She turns her head and I take that opportunity to trail my lips down her throat. Then I pick her up and carry her to bed, where I make her agree to no more animals while my face is between her thighs and she's on the brink of an orgasm.

Chapter 17

STICK-FIGURE FAMILIES AND HAPPILY EVER AFTERS

COURTNEY

"Do not cry," Abby says.

I focus on her in the mirror, giving her a watery smile.

"I'm not going to cry." I take a deep breath and let it out slowly so my tears don't make a liar out of me.

"Good, because you do not have time for the makeup artist to fix your face before it's time to get your ass down the aisle to that guy of yours."

"Is he okay?" I ask, turning away from the mirror.

"Last time I checked, he was pacing like you're going to run off—like you two don't already live together." She rolls her eyes.

I laugh. I can't help it. Lucas has gotten edgier and edgier as the wedding date's gotten closer. At first I thought he might be having second thoughts, but when I finally asked him about it he admitted that he was tired of waiting for me to become his wife. He tried to convince me to go to the courthouse and elope, but I had already spent months planning a wedding with Maddi and Abby. I refused to give in.

In the last ten months Lucas, Maddi, and I have settled into our life together with only a couple of hiccups along the way. The first hiccup was Lucas having to tell Maddi that Eva was moving back in with her boyfriend and that she wouldn't be around much. Thankfully, Maddi seemed to accept the news almost like she'd known it was coming—and was relieved by it. I don't know if it's good or bad, but Eva hasn't reached out to see Maddi since then. Honestly, I just feel sorry for Eva. She is missing out on watching her daughter grow up. One day, she will realize that and have regrets.

After Lucas brought up the idea of getting married, he officially proposed to me with a beautiful four-carat princess-cut diamond set in a simple platinum band. He slid the ring on my finger at dinner with his family and Abby there to watch. It was perfect—but not as perfect as my first unexpected proposal from Maddi, when she told me that we were *all* getting married.

I knew that he wanted us to get married before we moved into our new house, so I started planning our wedding, and we started planning our life. Part of that plan included us moving into his place while the house was being finished.

That was when our second hiccup happened, when Tom attempted to get in contact with me once again. He showed up at my apartment unannounced and drunk. It was on the day Lucas and I were moving me out of my place. Tom caused a huge scene, and we had to call the cops to escort him off the premises. He, like a drunken idiot, tried to get into a fight with Lucas. Then he resisted arrest and hit one of the officers. He spent the night in jail, and the next day his mom and dad came to the city to bail him out. They also came to see me, and to ask if Lucas would drop the charges he had pressed the night before. To say Lucas was not happy about their visit is an understatement, but he did agree to drop the charges if they promised to talk to their son about moving on with his life and making it clear that I was off-limits. They said they would, and I knew from the look on Lorie's face that she felt horrible about what happened. I wanted to hug her. I wanted to show her my ring and tell her how happy I was, but I didn't do that. We were simply no longer at that place. I have secretly sent her a few updates with photos through the mail, but that's as far as I will go to keep in touch with her.

Besides those couple of hitches, things have been good. Better than good.

Today I officially become Courtney Fremont, which means my good is only going to get better.

I sit down on the couch in the dressing room so that Abby can help me with my shoes.

I look up at the door when someone knocks lightly. "Come in."

Maddi walks in wearing a pale-pink tank dress with a hot-pink bow tied around her waist. Her dress is similar to Abby's strapless one—I asked both of them to be my bridesmaids today. Maddi had been with me all morning, but her grandmother came and got her about thirty minutes ago so she could go see Lucas.

"Hey, sweetheart. Everything okay?" I ask.

"Yes. Everyone is ready. The church looks so pretty."

"Even without the unicorns?" I ask.

She giggles. I think she suggested a unicorn theme every time we brought up planning—at first because she *actually* wanted me to have a unicorn-themed wedding, and later because she thought it was funny.

"I'm going to go outside to give you two a couple minutes together," Abby says when she's finished buckling the straps of my heels for me, which would have been impossible for me to do alone, since I can't see my feet under the poof of my dress.

"Sure." I nod at her, and she stands.

Then she leans down to kiss Maddi's cheek and tells her she's as pretty as a princess before leaving and shutting the door.

"I have something for you," Maddi says.

I notice then that she's holding a large wrapped package in both hands.

"Come sit with me." I pat the couch, and she sits down next to me and hands me the gift. I rest it on my lap, wondering what it is. It's heavy but thin, like a photo frame.

"What is it?" I ask.

"Your wedding present from me. Open it," she says.

I feel my face get soft, and tears start to sting the backs of my eyes.

"Sweetheart, you didn't have to get me anything."

"I made it a few weeks ago. When Grandma saw it she said I should give it to you," she tells me as I start to pull back the wrapping paper.

As soon as I have the paper off, I flip the sturdy frame over. My breath catches when I see the image behind the glass. It's a picture of a stick-figure family: a woman and a man with a little girl between them, all three holding hands, with a dog at their feet and a round sun in the sky overhead. Each of our names is written under our stick-figure legs. It's the most beautiful picture I have ever seen in my life.

My fingers trace over the lines of each of us in the picture, and tears fill my eyes. We're drawn into love—it's our family drawn on a simple piece of paper.

"I love it," I finally get out through the tightness in my throat. "It's so perfect. Thank you, sweetheart." I look up at her.

"You don't think it's dumb?"

"No." I set the frame near my feet, then turn to take her hands in mine. "It's not dumb. That picture is beautiful. You are beautiful. I'm so grateful that you've given me that, but I'm more thankful that you've given me a family in you and your dad. I love you both."

"I love you, too." I see her eyes start to get wet, and she looks away for a moment. "Can I ask you something?"

"Of course. Anything." I squeeze her hands.

"Can I . . . I mean, I know you're not . . . but after today can I maybe call you Mom?"

Oh god.

I choke down the sob I feel climb up the back of my throat as I pull her against me. "If you want that, then yes. I would love it if you called me Mom," I say. I hear her sniffle. "Thank you. Thank you for the gift, and for this moment. I promise I will cherish both of them forever," I tell her while cupping her soft cheeks. She nods, and I swipe away a tear that has fallen from her eye. "Is my makeup messed up?" I ask, wanting to change the mood. She looks at me, blinking away tears, then shakes her head no and smiles. "Good. Then are you ready for us to officially become a family?"

"Yes." She smiles brighter.

"Good." I hug her once more, then get up off the couch. I walk us both to the mirror and smile at our reflection. Thankfully, my makeup is still in place—otherwise Abby would have had to go hunt down the makeup artist for a quick touch-up.

"You look like a real-life princess," Maddi breathes.

I take in my strapless dress with a sweetheart neckline, an Empire waist, the same hot-pink sash as the girls have around my middle, and a big poofy skirt covered in millions of glittery pink and clear gems. I do look like a princess. Then again, Maddi is the one who picked my dress, because she said it looked like something a princess would wear. I wasn't sure about it when I saw it on the hanger, but once I had it on I knew it was the one for me. "I hope your dad likes it."

"Daddy is going to love it. He loves *you*, so he's going to love it." She takes my hand in hers, and once again I feel sorry for Eva. She is seriously missing out.

"You two ready?" Abby asks, poking her head in the door. I nod, pull in a breath, and then head out to marry the guy who changed my whole world.

"Mrs. Fremont, I swear to Christ if you don't get your sweet ass out here in two seconds, I'm coming in there to get you," I hear Lucas growl through the door of the hotel bathroom.

"Hold your horses." I grin at my reflection. Lucas has seen all my lingerie—he even said the bodysuit I had picked for him was worth the effort of taking it off me—but he's never seen me in something like this. My stomach fills with butterflies and I bite my bottom lip hard as I do another full-body scan. My eyes slide over my breasts, which are barely hidden under the sheer white lace bra I have on, and down to my sex, which is covered in the same sheer, thin white lace that has a slit for easy access cut into the material.

"I'm not fucking around, baby. Five . . . four . . . ," he says, starting to count down.

A thrill works down my spine. I know why he's impatient. We officially said "I do" this morning, then had a beautiful lunch with our friends and family. His mom and dad took Maddi home to his apartment, where they will be staying with her for the week. Then we caught a flight to Jamaica for our honeymoon.

He's been patient, but I could tell by the looks he was giving me when we were in the car on the way to the hotel that his patience was wearing thin. That's why I locked myself in the bathroom before I even looked around our hotel room.

I swing the bathroom door open when he gets to one. His eyes drop the length of me. I notice then that all he has on is a pair of boxers. "You know, Mr. Fremont, you're not very patient," I chide him.

His dark, hungry eyes meet mine.

"You're the most beautiful woman I have ever seen in my life," he states, taking a step toward me and wrapping his hand possessively around my hip. "I thought that the first time I saw you."

"You did?" I start to pant when his thumb slides along my hip bone, under the lace edge of my panties.

"I wanted to fuck you on the couch in my office. I went to bed night after night and jerked myself off to that fantasy," he growls, sliding a hand around to my back and then down to my ass. His other hand moves to cup my breast, his thumb skimming my nipple. "Fuck . . . the reality of you is better than anything I ever made up in my head."

"I would have let you . . . I mean, I would have let you fuck me on your couch," I tell him honestly as I rest my hands against his chest, then slide them up to his shoulders.

Without another word, he moves his hand from my breast to my other ass cheek, then both his hands glide down the backs of my thighs. He lifts me into his arms, and my legs circle his hips as he carries me away from the bathroom door and down a long hall, through a living room, and into the bedroom. A high four-poster bed is in the middle of the room, the door to the balcony is open, and the sea breeze coming in is causing the wispy white curtains around the bed to flutter. It looks like something from a movie set. He takes me to the bed and gets in on his knees, moving across the mattress with me still clinging to him. Once we are in the middle, he lays me down while keeping his weight off me.

His eyes scan my face, then down my body. They heat further when they reach the area between my legs. "Fuck, but I do like the way you think things through." His fingers slide down my stomach, over my pubic bone, and then through my folds—bare, since the panties do not have any material there. When his fingers run over my clit, my whole body jerks in response. "Already wet for me."

"I'm always wet for you."

"Mmm." He kisses me softly, then moves his lips down my neck, over my breasts—taking his time with each nipple—and down my stomach. He settles himself between my legs.

When his tongue finally touches my sex, I moan and my eyes fall closed. My fingers slip through his hair, and I hold on as he eats me like he has all the time in the world, bringing me close to the edge and then backing off.

My hips grind into his mouth, and my head digs into the pillow. "I'm so close," I whimper when he starts to suck on my clit. Before I can come, he pulls back. I fight the urge to cry out in distress. "Stop teasing me," I beg.

He pulls my clit back into his mouth, then suddenly fills me with two thick fingers. I come instantly. My back arches, and the heels of my feet dig into the mattress. My vision fills with stars. He leaves his fingers inside me, sliding in and out slowly, keeping my orgasm alive. I feel his lips touch my inner thigh before he kisses his way back up my body. When his mouth touches mine, I accept his kiss and open my mouth under his, tasting myself on his lips.

As his fingers leave my clit, he fills me with his cock, sinking into me slowly. I gasp against his mouth. There is nothing like being filled by him. There is nothing better than having all of him—and the connection I feel when he's inside me. His thrusts start off slow and steady before he speeds up, fucking me so hard that my back slides up the mattress.

"I love this pussy," he groans against my mouth.

My core contracts around his length as another orgasm starts to shimmer to the surface.

"Fuck. Give it to me, baby." He pulls on my bottom lip with his teeth, then bends his head and pulls my nipple into his mouth through the lace.

The sensation makes me fall apart. I come again—hard. I'm surprised by the intensity of it.

Before I have a chance to come down, he rolls us over so I'm on top. I whimper. "Lucas." My hips settle on either side of his. He was deep before—now he's so deep that it's almost too much for me to take.

"Ride me." His hands wrap around my hips, and he rocks me backward and forward.

I rest my hands against his chest and lift up, then fall. I do it hard. He moves his hands from my hips so one wraps around the back of my neck to pull me down for a deep kiss while the other slides between us so he can use his fingers on my clit again.

My pussy doesn't just tighten, it clenches almost painfully.

"Too much," I pant, rocking and falling against him.

"No. You've got another in you—and I want it," he growls, rolling my clit faster.

Somehow my body gives in, and another orgasm washes over me. This one almost makes me black out. Both his hands move to my hips, and he lifts me two more times, thrusting up every time he jerks me down. I listen to him groan through his orgasm, and I fall against his chest, breathing heavy. I hear him breathing the same way. Both our bodies are damp with perspiration. He wraps me in his arms, and I settle my face in the crook of his neck.

I don't remember anything else, because two seconds later I fall asleep on top of him with him still inside me. I know there is no place I'd rather be.

∼

I wake to the smell of the ocean, the sound of waves crashing against the shore, and the feel of a cool breeze against my bare skin. I slowly blink my eyes open. A smile curves my lips when I see the view. Even from the bed, I can see the white sands of the beach, the clear blue waters of the ocean, and Lucas standing at the edge of that ocean in nothing but a pair of board shorts. He's so perfect it almost hurts to look at him. He's toned, not overly muscular, and the last week under the Jamaican sun has given him a golden tan.

I sit up, bringing the thin sheet with me. Then I move to the edge of the bed and get up. I pad to the door of the balcony and look out. We splurged on this place when we decided where to go for our honeymoon. It cost a ton for a suite with a private stretch of beach, but it's so worth it. I'm going to miss this place when we leave tomorrow to go home. It has been nice having time alone together. We haven't done much—we've spent most of our time in bed or right outside our door on the beach, lazing in the sun, relaxing, chatting, and laughing. As nice as it's been to connect with Lucas the way we have over the past few days, though, I miss our girl. I know he does, too.

As if he senses me watching him, his eyes come to me. A small smile spreads across his face. I wait for him as he walks across the beach and then up the stairs that lead to our balcony. When he reaches me, he tugs the sheet from my grasp, gathers me in his arms, and carries me back to bed. He makes love to me.

I open my eyes and look up into Lucas's beautiful eyes when I feel his fingers trail down my back. "You okay?" I ask, sounding sleepy even though I just woke up a little over an hour ago. Then again, he did just give me two great orgasms.

"I hate that we gotta leave here tomorrow, but I miss Maddi."

"I miss her, too," I agree. "Next time we'll bring her with us."

"She'd like that." His fingers skim up my back, then move at random on my spine.

"Mmm." I snuggle closer to him.

Suddenly I'm not pressed to his side any longer, I'm on my back, and his mouth is covering mine. The kiss is deep and hard. I know he's saying something, I just don't know what it is.

"Fuck, but I really fucking love you," he says when he pulls away. I start to open my mouth but stop when he continues. "I thought I lost my shot at this when I screwed up and married Eva. I never thought I'd have what we have, never thought that I would be as happy as I am. You changed everything in my world."

Holy crap.

I breathe in deep, but it doesn't seem to be helping.

"You've given me back my dream, baby. Given me back the life I always wanted—a good woman, a solid family. Thank you."

"You're going to make me cry," I whisper, cupping his stubbled jaw.

"Please don't." He smiles. "I just want you to know that the things that are important to you are the same things that are important to me. Family. You, Maddi, and me."

"And Merida?" I swallow back tears.

"Yeah, and Merida," he agrees softly.

He slides back inside me and makes love to me once more.

Later that night, lying in the crook of his arm, watching the moonlight reflect off the ocean, I say a silent thank-you for the man next to me, the little girl who holds my heart, and the family I always wanted. Because of them, I know that dreams do come true.

Epilogue

COURTNEY

Three years later

"Mrs. Fremont?" Dr. Christine Hoffman smiles at me as she comes into the room. "Michelle said you haven't been feeling well. What seems to be the issue?"

"I'm not sure." I tuck my hands between my thighs to warm my fingers. "I keep getting headaches, and I feel tired all the time no matter how much sleep I get."

"When was your last period?" she asks, taking my temp and then looking in my ears.

"Last month. I'm not pregnant. I don't know what's wrong with me, but I do know it's not that. My ex-husband and I tried for years to get pregnant. We even tried IVF, but it never worked. The specialist I went to told me after five rounds of IVF that I would never have a child."

She nods in understanding. "Lean back for me." I lie back on the table, hearing the paper crunch under me. She lifts my shirt and pulls down the leggings I have on. She pushes down just above my pubic bone and feels around on my stomach before jotting something down. "Do you mind taking a blood and urine test?"

"No. Do you think everything is okay?"

"I'm sure everything is fine. I just want to check your numbers to make sure that everything is where it should be."

"Okay," I agree.

"Go use this in the bathroom in the hall. Just leave it on the counter." She hands me a clear plastic cup. "Michelle will be in after to take your blood. Once I get the results, I'll give you a call."

"Sounds good. Thank you." I give her another smile before she leaves the room.

I go pee in the cup, then leave it where she told me to and head back to the room. Once there, I hop back up on the table and pull my cell phone out of my purse. I send a text to Lucas to ask what he wants to do for dinner. He's been responsible for cooking for the last month, since Maddi has swim at the local YMCA. Her practice and meets normally last until six fifteen, meaning we don't get home until close to six thirty, depending on if the swim meet is away or at home.

Dinner?

We'll order in Chinese. You want your usual? How's work?

I bite my lip. I didn't tell him I had a doctor's appointment today. He worries about me and Maddi all the time. I know it's because he loves us and wants to protect us, but if he keeps going the way he is he's going to have a heart attack from the stress.

Work is good. I'll be home by five to change before heading over to the school.

Okay baby, call me when you're home and I'll see you girls when you get home tonight.

KK Love you.

I press "Send" and smile when his next text comes up on the screen.

Love you more.

I drop my phone back into my bag, then pick up one of the office magazines to keep myself busy.

A few minutes later, Michelle comes in and takes my blood. Just when I'm about to walk out of the room, Dr. Hoffman stops me at the door.

"Take a seat for me, Courtney," she says, looking at me oddly.

I nod and get back up on the table.

"Is everything okay?"

"I think so." She takes a seat on a rolling chair, then slides across the floor toward me.

"What does that mean?"

"You're pregnant."

I stare at her, not sure I heard her right. Actually, I'm *sure* I didn't hear her right.

"On occasion a woman can mistake implantation bleeding for her period." I continue to stare at her. "Are you okay?"

I think I might be in shock. I can't seem to get my brain and mouth to work the way they should be working. "Did you . . . did you say I'm *pregnant?*"

"Yes. I'm still going to run your blood test just to confirm, but your urine test came out positive for pregnancy."

"How? How is that possible?"

"I have no answer for you, especially after your history. I can say that god works in mysterious ways from time to time."

I rest my hand against my stomach, feeling both happy and totally freaked out. "I'm pregnant."

"You are. As soon as we have the blood results back, you will have confirmation, but I did two urine tests, and both came back with a positive response immediately. I've never had one of those tests be a false positive—definitely not two of them."

"Maybe something is wrong with my urine. Or maybe it was someone else's urine?"

"We are not in the business of leaving random urine samples lying around the office, so that's not possible." She smiles. "I can understand your disbelief, given your history, but I hope this is good news."

"This isn't good news." I shake my head, feeling my throat start to get tight with tears. "This is the *best* news I've ever heard in my life. I . . . I never thought . . ."

"I know." She smiles gently as tears wet my cheeks. "I'm happy for you."

"Thank you." I wipe my face with the tissues she hands me.

"I'll have the blood results by tomorrow morning. Until then, just relax. The first trimester is one of the hardest. Your body is going through a million changes while it figures out how to give life to the life inside of you."

Relax? I won't be able to relax until the baby is in my arms.

Holy cow. A baby. Lucas and I are having a baby. Maddi is going to be a big sister.

"I'll try to relax," I lie.

She gives me a knowing smile, then stands. "I'll have Michelle give you the number for a doctor who's a friend of mine before you leave. She'll take great care of you and the baby."

"Thank you," I whisper.

She surprises me by giving me a hug, then heads out of the room.

I don't know how long I sit there looking down at my hand resting on my stomach, but it's a while before I get up and leave the office. I make sure to get the referral number from Michelle before I go.

LUCAS

My eyes go over the back of the couch and zero in on Courtney as she moves around the kitchen, putting away dishes and cleaning up the mess she and Maddi made baking cookies for Maddi's swim team. For the last few weeks, she hasn't been herself. I haven't figured out what it is, but she's been off. When I've asked her about it, she's told me she's fine or that she's just tired or has a headache. I'm trying not to let it get to me too much, but the last time she started acting strange she tried to leave me.

Today she seems to be living in her head. It's odd. She's still happy, still affectionate, but she's different. I just can't put my finger on how. All I know is I don't like it.

"Baby, leave that stuff. I'll do it later. Come hang with me and watch a show," I call to her.

Her eyes meet mine. "I'm almost done."

She continues doing what she's doing. I growl under my breath, then set my beer down on the coffee table and get up off the couch. I head right for the fridge and grab a bottle of wine, pour her a glass, then grab her hand and start pulling her with me toward the living room.

"Lucas, what are you doing?" She tugs at my hand, but I don't let up on the hold I've got on her.

"You're gonna sit with me, drink a glass of wine, and watch a show."

"I can't," she says.

I look at her. "You can't, or you won't? What's going on?"

"I . . . Nothing?" She shakes her head, and the freaked-out look in her eyes makes my hackles rise.

"Something is up?"

"Nothing is up. I was just cleaning the kitchen."

"Yeah, and I told you I'd do it after we spent some time together." I sit on the couch and pull her down with me. "Here." I hold the glass out to her, and she looks at it like it's going to sprout fangs and strike out at her.

"I can't have that."

"Why not?" I ask. Her eyes widen. "Courtney, if you don't start talking to me, I'm going to lose my fucking mind. Tell me what the fuck is going on."

"You know, you're annoying," she snaps, glaring at me.

"You say that a lot. Yet you still agreed to marry me, and you're still married to me."

"Well, today you're more annoying than ever."

"Talk to me," I growl.

Her eyes narrow even further. "Fine, ruin it. I'm pregnant. Are you happy now?"

She falls back against the back of the couch while my mouth drops open and my stomach gets tight.

"I wanted to surprise you with the news, but no"—she shakes her head—"of course you couldn't let me do that, could you? You just had to be all annoying and demanding and ruin it."

She has to gasp the word *it* against my lips, because I crash my mouth down on hers. I thread the fingers of one of my hands through her hair, then rest my other hand over her flat stomach. Over our child. I kiss her with everything I'm feeling. I'm overwhelmed with happiness, overwhelmed with surprise, but mostly overwhelmed with love.

"You're really *pregnant*?" I ask when I pull my mouth from hers. She nods. "Fuck. Fuck me." I rest my forehead against hers. "When did you find out?"

"Today," she says.

I lean back and frown down at her.

"I didn't want you to worry, which is what you always do, so I didn't tell you that I had an appointment. I've been feeling off. I thought something might be wrong, and—"

"Do not ever do that again." I cut her off. "I know you think I worry too much, but I love you and Maddi. You two make up my world. If you ever feel like something is wrong, I want you to tell me."

"I'm sorry." She bites her bottom lip. "The good news is, nothing is wrong. What I've been feeling is normal during the first trimester."

"Yeah, that's good news." My hand rubs her stomach. "So you found out today?"

"Yes. The doctor did two urine tests, and they both came back positive. She said the blood test will be back in the morning for double confirmation."

"We're having a baby," I whisper, looking into her eyes.

She smiles, and her face softens. "We're having a baby." Her hand cups my cheek. "Maddi is going to be a big sister. Do you think she will be happy?"

"I know she will be," I say, watching her smile.

"I want to at least surprise *her* with the news, since you ruined the surprise I had in mind for you."

"What was my surprise?"

"Now you'll never know, since you ruined it."

"Fine." I nip her bottom lip, and she laughs.

Her body seems to melt under mine. "I love you, Lucas."

"I love you, too, baby. Always," I whisper.

"Always," she whispers back.

～

MADELINE

"I'm ready for a story, Mom and Dad," I yell downstairs. I check on my hamster, Beanie, and my guinea pig, Walter, then get into my big bed. It's a double that I picked out when we moved into the house. I love the house and I love my bedroom, but I really love my bed because it's big enough for my dad, mom, me, and Merida to cuddle on for story time. My friend Susie told me I'm too old to have my parents read me books at night and tuck me in. I told her she's stupid. Until I go to college, I'm going to have my dad and mom tuck me in and read to me. Anyway, they don't think I'm too old.

"Did you brush your teeth?" Dad asks, coming into the room holding Mom's hand.

I don't roll my eyes—even though I want to—but I see Mom roll hers.

"Yes." I giggle.

"Good. Scoot to the middle," he says. They get into bed on either side of me, but Merida doesn't move from her spot at my feet.

"I can't wait to see what happens next in the story," I say, holding up the book we have been reading for the last two weeks. It's a book about a girl who's a princess warrior on a mission to save her people from an evil witch.

"Tonight we have something else to read," Mom tells me.

I frown. We've been reading the princess book for weeks now. It's almost done.

"What book?"

"This one."

She hands me a book, and I look at the cover.

The picture looks like the stick-figure family I drew for her a long time ago, which she hung just inside the front door of the house as soon as we moved in. I read the title: Madeline Becomes a Big Sister. My stomach suddenly feels funny, like a million worms are squirming around inside it.

"Open it and read it to us, honey," Dad says.

I open to the first page and read out loud, then turn and read the second, then the third. On the fourth page, I stop and look between my parents. "I'm going to be a big sister?"

"Yes!" they both say at the same time.

"I'm *really* going to be a big sister?" I get up on my knees and turn around to look at both of them.

"Yes." Mom laughs, and Dad smiles.

"Oh my god!" I shout, standing up on my bed. I jump up and down, making Merida hop off onto the floor. "I'm going to have a baby brother."

"Well, we don't know what we are having yet." Mom grins.

I smile, then jump again.

"I'm going to have a baby brother or sister!" I yell.

"I take it you're happy," Dad says.

I fall on top of him and hug him as hard as I can.

"Yes, so happy."

"Good." He kisses the top of my head. When he lets me go, I hug Mom, but I do it more carefully.

"I love you, sweetheart," she whispers.

Just like every time she tells me she loves me or calls me sweetheart, my chest gets warm.

"I love you, too." I rest against her side, then touch her stomach and smile.

~

A little under nine months later, Luke Edward Fremont came into the world. Upon his arrival, his sister drew a new family portrait that included him. She also made sure that in the picture he was crying, since he seemed to do that a lot.

~

LORIE

As soon as I see the yellow envelope in my mailbox, my hands shake with excitement. I pull it out and tuck it under my arm, then go through the rest of the mail as I head into the house. It's mostly junk mail, which I toss on the kitchen island. I head down the hall toward my office. I go right to my desk and take a seat, smiling. These updates are few and far between. Each one hurts, but they also help with the loss I suffered more than four years ago. With a deep breath, I carefully open the flap of the envelope and pull out the single photo inside. Tears instantly fill my eyes. My beautiful girl. She looks so happy, so content tucked under her husband's arm with a very chubby boy on her hip, a beautiful almost-teenage girl leaning into her opposite side, and a very ugly dog at their feet.

"I'm happy for you. Happy that you found your family," I tell the image before I carefully put the picture back in the envelope and tuck it away with the rest of the letters I've gotten over the last few years. Once I'm done, I leave my office and head to the kitchen to make dinner for myself. I do it smiling.

Three years ago, I did something I never would have had the courage to do before I watched Courtney stand up for herself. I left my husband and moved into my own place, and I have never been happier.

About the Author

Aurora Rose Reynolds is a *New York Times* and *USA Today* bestselling author whose wildly popular series include Until, Until Him, Until Her, Underground Kings, and Fluke My Life.

Her writing career started in an attempt to get the outrageously alpha men who resided in her head to leave her alone, and it has blossomed into an opportunity to share her stories with readers all over the world.

For more information on Reynolds's latest books or to connect with her, contact her on Facebook at www.facebook.com/AuthorAuroraRoseReynolds or on Twitter @Auroraroser, or via email at Auroraroser@gmail.com. To order signed books and find out the latest news, visit her at www.AuroraRoseReynolds.com or https://www.goodreads.com/Auroraroser